Praise for *Dreams of Bali*

"*Dreams of Bali* is a worthwhile read with its engaging plot and intriguing characters. I had to keep on reading to find out what was going to happen next. Harte did not disappoint."
—*Just About Write*

By the Author

Dreams of Bali

Magic of the Heart

MAGIC
OF THE HEART

by

C.J. Harte

2010

MAGIC OF THE HEART
© 2010 By C.J. Harte. All Rights Reserved.

ISBN 10: 1-60282-131-3
ISBN 13: 978-1-60282-131-6

This Trade Paperback Original Is Published By
Bold Strokes Books, Inc.
P.O. Box 249
Valley Falls, NY 12185

First Edition: January 2010

CREDITS
EDITORS: CINDY CRESAP AND STACIA SEAMAN
PRODUCTION DESIGN: STACIA SEAMAN
COVER DESIGN BY SHERI (GRAPHICARTIST2020@HOTMAIL.COM)

Acknowledgments

This book would not be in print if not for the vision, determination, and encouragement of Len Barot and Bold Strokes Books. Len made Bold Strokes a home for lots of wonderful writers. I'm fortunate to be included in that group. Cindy Cresap survived being my editor and still has hair. Thank you for your patience. My beta readers provided me immeasurable guidance in shaping the story. Thank you to Bett and Carla, Pam S, Pam F, Sandy, Glenda, Joan, and Gis.

I need to thank the wonderful members of the Rainbow Writer's group who read, reread, and reread various versions and helped to make the story a better one. Their critiques and insights were invaluable.

Finally, I want to thank Giselle for encouraging my writing, being such a great friend, and putting up with my Maggie.

Dedication

To Maggie, who inspired my writing.
Thank you for being in my life
and sharing your short life with me.

CHAPTER ONE

Maggie stared out the window at the gazebo. Sun and shadows danced across the empty structure. It was another sunny California day in early November. She pulled her arms around herself as if to keep the emptiness from growing any larger. She imagined what it would feel like to sit out there holding hands with a lover. "Not likely. Not anytime soon," she whispered. The only way to fight that feeling was to push those thoughts away. She stared at the gazebo and restored the feeling of calm. "It's not fucking fair."

"What's not fair, M.J.?" The quiet solitude was broken by Maya Browning, her personal assistant, who came in carrying a bunch of notes.

"Life. Nothing." Maggie kept her personal and professional lives very separate. "What's up?" Business problems were easier to solve and didn't usually require much commitment.

Maya looked at her feet. Maggie could feel the mood changing and she slid on her business persona as easily as she put on her shoes. "What's going on?"

Maya finally looked up, took a deep breath, and spoke. "We need to redo some of the tracks on the new CD."

She felt the calm slipping away and there was little she could do to stop it. "What the fuck do you mean we need to redo?"

"Look, M.J., we've been trying to fix it."

"Trying doesn't cut it. Only results. What the hell happened?" She was M.J. Carson, the superstar. She knew how to charm, how to entertain, how to get whatever or whomever she wanted. These were skills she used to survive and advance her career. Being charming was a second skin she could slip on easily. Today, however, wasn't one of those times. "Shit, Maya, these tracks were supposed to be done two months ago, before we begin the damn tour." She paced around her home office. "I'm supposed to leave tonight. When the hell is this supposed to get done?"

"Look, M.J., the music will be done in time. Don't worry."

"Don't worry?" Maggie stared at her, not believing what she was hearing. "Who the fuck should worry? It's only my name and voice."

Maya spoke calmly. "We can have it done by the end of the month and to the distributor before Christmas. I promise."

Maggie shook her head. This was so damn typical. "When I was sixteen and playing anywhere I could get a gig, I expected things to get screwed up. Once the band became a success, I hired people to make sure that never happened so I could concentrate on writing and performing music. Not managing it. Damn it, Maya, that's your job. You've worked for me for five years and here I am, after nearly twenty years in the business, and things are fucked up. Do I have to do everything?" She shook her head. *I definitely need a break.* "You knew this album needed to be getting big play before the tour. You knew what a tight deadline we're working on. You knew how hard I've worked to get these songs written and the music put together. You knew how difficult it was to round everyone up to get the recording done in the first place. You knew I wanted to spend the next three weeks with the kids. Why the hell am I just finding out it hasn't been finished?"

Maya looked at her notes. "When we originally listened to the master, there were some rough places. The sound engineer wasn't sure what caused it but thought he could fix it." She looked up. "He called me this morning and said there was no way to fix it. It's only a small portion of a couple of tracks. No big deal. It'll be done on time."

Maggie walked over to the window overlooking the sun-dappled gazebo. She could barely resurrect any of the threads of peace she felt earlier. *Another fucking sunny day*, she thought. She turned to face Maya. "No big deal? No fucking big deal! Have you forgotten who will put in the long hours recording in some damn cramped studio? Are you the one paying for the redo? Are you going to listen to the gripes from the band when we call them in? Again." Maggie didn't wait for an answer. "Don't you dare tell me not to worry. Call Karl and tell him to get the same mixers from the last CD. Fly them out if we have to. I don't want anyone else and I don't care how much. Understand?"

Maya nodded. "I'll make sure it's done."

Maggie wanted to scream or throw something. She felt like a cat about to pounce. She repeated her warning. "Do you understand?"

Maya nodded. "I understand."

"Go on. Get out. I need to finish packing." Before Maya had a chance to exit, Maggie stopped her. "Oh, by the way, are you sure all the arrangements have been made for this trip? I don't want any hassles for the next three weeks. And no media!"

"Your itinerary is with your tickets," Maya said. "I'll have the recording set up for three weeks from tomorrow. We'll record in Orlando."

"Thanks, Maya. I don't know how I'd manage without you."

"Yeah, sure. Have a great trip." Maya left quickly.

Finally alone, Maggie sat in front of the window and stared out at the garden. The office faced the eastern edge of her estate and provided a languorous, peaceful view of the large natural-wood gazebo nestled among the shade trees. The solitude and beauty of the structure was the deciding factor when they purchased the place seven years ago, and the reason this room had become her office. The gazebo stood as a silent sentinel, a symbol of the peace and quiet she rarely experienced in her own life.

She sighed. "Another fucking sunny day."

CHAPTER TWO

Susan Hettinger quickly slid into her seat in first class, allowing other passengers to board the plane. She wondered what had happened to her life. There was a time when she was first starting out that she had felt more in control. Lately she seemed to be spending more time on planes, less time with her family, and she had zero personal life. She leaned her head against the seat and watched as an attractive woman with two children took the remaining seats in her row, with the daughter sitting next to her.

Shortly after take-off, the girl asked, "Are you going to Disney World too?"

For the first time that day, Susan smiled. "Not anytime soon, I'm afraid. I live in Orlando."

"My mom is taking us on a vacation. Do you have a little girl?"

Susan thought about her own daughter and how little time she had spent with her recently. "I do. Her name is Cady and she is four years old. How old are you?" *Note to self: I need to spend more time with Cady.*

"I'm Beth and I'm seven. That's my brother D.J. over there. He's three. And that's my mom." She pointed to the woman and little boy. "I'm the oldest."

The flight attendant interrupted their conversation, offering something to drink and getting dinner orders.

I can't believe the office wasn't able to get a direct flight. She sipped her diet soda and hoped she could stay awake.

She leaned her seat back and let her mind drift. When was the last time she had relaxed, really relaxed? She went back more than six years to a time when she was a rising star accountant at a major accounting firm. She'd shared her ideas with colleagues who recognized her creativity and organization. That was before Ed Turner offered her the job as his chief financial officer in his venture company in the entertainment industry. Sometimes she felt her life had been in a steady decline ever since.

When she first started the job, Susan loved to say, "I work in the entertainment industry." Suddenly she was much more interesting. People quizzed her incessantly about whom she knew and what gossip she'd heard. When she finally explained that she was the financial manager for a creative projects agency, people quickly lost interest—unless they were trying to plead for more money for their projects or they were caught doing something shady. Then their language was much less pleasant. These creative people all too often liked to use their creativity with other people's money, and it was her job to keep track of every cent spent.

The overhead announcement interrupted her thoughts. She tightened her seat belt and reminded herself that she was a working single parent who managed a team of professionals handling over $100 million in projects a year. Since no one except the producers and backers cared about what she did, she no longer tried to explain her job to strangers, or her family, and no longer felt the need to impress anyone. She just introduced herself as an accountant and avoided the tedious questioning. And it kept her life routine…and boring.

As she stared at the magazine she'd bought in the airport, she admitted that she would barely recognize who was number one on the Billboard charts or who starred in the top-flight movies. At times she thought she should pay more attention to who was on the A-list, especially when Ed was ranting about some deal with some star. At least she could pretend to know what they were talking about. How had her life become so boring? So repetitive. *Well, Susan, that's the way you wanted your life. It's probably going to take something big to change it.*

The sound of children's laughter interrupted her thoughts. Beth was holding on to a game board. D.J. could barely reach across the aisle. By the time he finally moved his piece on the board, someone walked down the aisle and he had to struggle to keep his seat. His last effort landed him on the floor and caused his sister to giggle.

Smiling, Susan asked, "Would you two like to get a little closer?"

"I'm sorry if my children are bothering you."

When the mother spoke, Susan heard the tingling notes of a warm springtime melody. Just a hint of amusement and a measure of promise. Susan turned to face the speaker. Sitting across the aisle was an attractive brunette near her own age. Susan was impressed by the gentle way the woman dealt with the disgruntled child. It was when the woman looked up and smiled that Susan felt a rush of unexpected heat.

"They're not a problem," Susan said. "I think he just wants to play." Seeing the disappointed look on D.J.'s face, Susan said, "Look, why don't we trade seats for a while? It would be a lot more fun if they could play the game."

"Are you sure? That's very generous of you."

Once they were settled next to each other, the mother said, "My name is Margaret Carson-Baxter, but my friends call me Maggie."

Susan accepted the outstretched hand. Maggie's hand was surprisingly large and strong. Susan found her concentration slipping as her blood warmed turning into liquid honey. She stared up into beautiful, laughing eyes. Suddenly she was having trouble remembering anything, much less what was being said. She stumbled over her own name. "Susan, uh, Susan, uh, Hettinger." She chastised herself for this sudden inability to start a conversation. *I must be tired.*

Maggie didn't seem to notice any awkwardness. "I usually get nonstop flights," she said, "but this was the only flight leaving when I wanted to leave. The next flight wasn't until ten. I wouldn't mind, but my kids would probably sleep part of the way and then be wound up once we landed." Maggie smiled. "Two kids going at a hundred twenty miles per hour at five in the morning is not healthy for mom or kids."

Susan laughed and thought of her own daughter's antics. "My office did the same thing, scheduling me on this flight. This time I wanted to be home before I was doing the same thing." Susan found herself relaxing. "Your children are beautiful, like their mother." She sat back abruptly. "Oh, my God, I can't believe I said that."

Maggie laughed and touched Susan's arm. "Thank you. That's the nicest compliment I've had in a long time. I think my children are beautiful, but it's always nice to hear it from others."

"I...I..." Susan tried to find some appropriate response that would keep her foot out of her mouth. "I guess most parents think that. I love when my coworkers say something nice about my daughter. Of course, families are often a topic of conversation at work." *God, Susan, how lame is that? You never join office conversations unless it deals with business.*

Maggie couldn't remember talking about children with any of her co-workers. Maya was a lesbian. Her other two assistants weren't married. Karl was married, but she didn't know whether or not he had kids. That fact surprised her. "I guess so." Maggie didn't want to do any further exploration of that topic. "I think I need to go to the restroom."

Susan watched Maggie walk down the aisle. She was tall and solid with a walk that was both confident and easy. Everything spoke of reserve and control. Still, there was something compelling about her. When Maggie returned, Susan felt herself falling back into the easy conversation.

"Where are you headed to?" Maggie asked.

"I live in Orlando. Your daughter mentioned that you folks are heading to Disney. Guess we'll be on the same flight all the way."

"That was another reason for wanting to get into Orlando early. The kids have been absolutely wild since I told them we were going." Maggie's tone became softer when she spoke about her children. "This is a combination of business and pleasure. I haven't had a vacation with the kids in a long time. To be honest, I don't think I've had a real vacation in the last two years."

"I try to set aside special time for my daughter." *Susan, that was a really smart thing to say.* "What I mean is that I make sure I take the weekend off when I have to be away during the week. They grow so fast, and I don't want to miss any part of her life."

"Derek and I feel the same way."

"Derek?" Susan wasn't sure she was ready for the answer.

"My husband. He's a professional football player and has a game this weekend. He won't be able to join us until right before Christmas."

Maggie mentioned his name and Susan nodded. "Oh, Derek Baxter." While Susan was sure her father would have recognized the name, she did not follow the sport. Or, for that matter, any sport. For once she wished she had.

"I'm heading home," Susan said. "I've been in California all week on business." Realizing she had put herself in a corner, she dreaded the next question.

"What do you do?"

Susan groaned and gave her well-rehearsed answer. "I'm the accounting director for a business in Orlando. What do you do?" Maggie's eyes hadn't glazed over, but Susan didn't want to give her the chance to say, "How nice."

"I'm in music." Maggie hesitated. "Mostly producing." Maggie wasn't sure how much more to reveal.

"You must have to deal with a lot of men. I had a good friend in college who was determined to succeed as a symphony director. She struggled for a long time and then decided to just compose. Even that was difficult. She now teaches at Florida State."

Maggie smiled. This was one of her favorite topics. "Do you realize how few women conduct major symphonies or head major recording studios? And women composers haven't gotten the financing men have. It doesn't matter the genre. Where are the women? Sure, there are a few, but not nearly enough." Maggie paused and realized she had revealed too much. "Sorry. My senior paper in college was on the role of women in music management and administration."

"Don't apologize. Women still have many glass ceilings to break." Susan searched for some clever thing to say. "What do you think it will take to make that change?" *Clever, really clever, Susan!* While it got the desired response and Maggie continued talking, Susan was suddenly aware of how much she was enjoying the conversation and didn't want their time together to end.

Fate intervened when the plane landed in Dallas for their only stop. First they were delayed for two hours while the airline tried to fix a leaky faucet, unsuccessfully. Next they were told the plane was not flyable. Finally, the airlines recruited another plane, at another gate, in another terminal. When the airline offered her VIP assistance including a waiting electric cart, Maggie grabbed Susan's arm. "Come on. Why walk when we can ride?" Kids, carry-ons, and two adults were quickly moved to the awaiting cart and zoomed to the new gate.

Susan had never had such great service, except for the time she broke her foot. She briefly wondered if Maggie was some airline VIP but then erased that thought with the acknowledgment of the assistance being designed for the kids. They were all settled in their first-class seats before their flying companions were embarking from the Sky Train at the terminal.

Once aboard the plane and headed to Orlando, Maggie

discovered her wallet was missing. "Damn, all my identification is in it. It had to have fallen out on the other plane."

One of the flight attendants noticed Maggie's agitation and came up. "May we help you, Ms. Carson?" The attendant's inquiries were not helpful. "A member of the cleaning crew may have picked it up," the attendant said. "I am sure we'll find it. Do you need to make a call or other arrangements?"

Frustration evident, Maggie nonetheless remained gracious. "Ms. Carson," the attendant whispered, "could I get your autograph for my nephew?"

Her husband must be some star quarterback, Susan thought, as Maggie asked the nephew's name and signed her name. Susan thought Maggie was vaguely familiar, but she quickly discarded that thought when she realized she had been staring at Maggie all evening. *Of course she's familiar looking. Susan, this is not like you.* Sitting back in her seat, she tried to calm her racing heart. *Come on, Susan, this is some married stranger. Chill,* she reminded herself. *An attractive married stranger. Admit it, you haven't enjoyed being with another woman this much in a long, long, long time. What is it about Maggie? This is like the time I went to a circus and watched the magician pull rabbits and other wonderful objects out of the hat. But Maggie is a married magical person. Oh, shit.*

It was nearly three in the morning when the plane finally landed in Orlando and they found their way to the baggage claim to wait for the bags. "My car is parked in the terminal lot. If you need a ride or if I can help with anything..." Susan let the sentence fall off. What else could she offer? Maggie obviously was financially secure...and married, she again reminded herself.

"Susan, thank you. I have a rental car and hotel arranged. Oh, shit. I forgot. I don't have my wallet."

Before her brain could get in gear, Susan opened her mouth. "I have my car here and I have a large house with plenty of room. You're welcome to stay until you can work something out." When her brain caught up with her mouth it screamed. *What are you doing, Miss Obsessive-Compulsive Queen of Privacy?* "I have only one child and it's a really large house." *Great, that's a winning argument!*

"Are you sure you don't mind?"

"Of course I'm sure. Guests are always welcome at my house." *Right, and it is going to snow in Orlando tomorrow. You've really gone and done it now.*

Maggie rubbed her sleeping son's back. She quickly reviewed all her options before she made a decision. "Okay, but only if you let me buy dinner when I get some money."

Maggie's lopsided smile was worth it. Susan's heart threatened to stop beating. She took another deep breath, sealed the agreement with a handshake, and herded Maggie and her children into the waiting car. Considering the amount of luggage Maggie and her kids had, Susan was glad she had a minivan.

As they drove away from the airport, panic finally set in. Susan realized she had no idea what kind of person Maggie was, where she lived, how she lived, how much money she earned. She figured Maggie's husband earned a six- or seven-figure—*but who's counting*—salary. Still, she was bringing a total stranger to her modest home in Winter Park, a conservative, upper-middle-income area north of Orlando. A place no one outside her family had ever stayed.

Susan's house once belonged to her parents but was given to her when her father retired and her parents started traveling. The older neighborhood was composed of many old friends of her parents as well as an increasing number of young upwardly mobile families with children, looking for the "right" starter address. When her father died, Susan's mom came back to live in the mother-in-law cottage behind her house and to care for

Susan's daughter during Susan's frequent out-of-town business trips.

❖

Susan used the remote control to open the garage door. As she drove into the garage, a nagging parental voice reminded her of her lifestyle, her responsibilities, and her near dread of meeting new people. Now, she'd spent the entire trip entranced with a stranger and brought Maggie and her children into her house. *Me, the queen of...no, don't go there. Well, as Scarlett O'Hara would say, "I'll think about that tomorrow."*

The sleeping children were carried in and quickly settled into the spare beds in Cady's room. Cady stirred briefly but fell back asleep. Unloading the car was a quest to defy gravity and other laws of physics. Somehow they managed to get everything into the house in one trip. "You're a lifesaver," Maggie said.

Susan felt both awkward and guilty. Awkward because of her need to continue the connection with Maggie. Guilty for the feelings of attraction. Her control slipping, she mumbled something.

Maggie reached for Susan's arm. "Susan, I'm serious. I can't tell you how much all this means to me. Thank you."

Maggie's hand heated the skin on Susan's arm. A subtle tremor began in the center of Susan's body and threatened to spread. Susan willed her body to stay still. After Maggie let go, Susan felt unexpectedly empty.

Everything changed once they moved into the room that served as Susan's home office. The white enameled daybed was now the resting place of many late-night reports. The computer sat quietly. The whole room was a silent testimony to her structured, organized life. *My boring. organized life.*

"I'm sorry the room is such a mess," Susan said as she grabbed a stack of papers. "I leave all my folders out so I can return to them when I get home." Looking around at the carefully arranged and color-coordinated stacks of working files, she realized she had a whole Southern Forest in processed paper. *Oh, goddess, suppose she's one of those rabid West Coast environmentalists.* There was no way to suddenly make all the paper disappear unless Susan began shoveling it under her clothes. Briefly she wondered if Maggie would notice if she tried to hide the paper under her blouse.

Maggie was clearly amused at Susan's scurrying. "You can organize my office any day. Yours looks so neat. I have to rely on my assistant to help me figure out what I do each day." Susan didn't care if Maggie was an environmentalist. She was willing to start a paperless work system if Maggie approved.

As they cleared the room, Maggie asked, "If it wouldn't be a problem, I'd love some hot tea. Anything herbal or caffeine free. Then if you can point me to a hot shower, I'll be eternally in your debt."

There was a small half-bath off the family room. Another full-size bathroom was located near Cady's bedroom, next to the spare bedroom in which her mother slept. The pipes in that bathroom made lovely noises that were loud enough to stir the neighborhood. *Why haven't I gotten that fixed?* That left only the bathroom in Susan's bedroom. She had little choice. *Why did I invite this person into my house? Well, it's a little late to worry about that now.* The voices continued to argue. *Shut up!* Susan finally ordered her overactive imagination.

She grabbed towels and led Maggie into her bathroom. "If you don't mind using the shower in my bedroom, you can go ahead and clean up there while I fix us both some tea."

"Perfect." Maggie reached for Susan's arm as she walked by. "Susan, you have been great. If you're uncomfortable about anything, it's okay. I can wait until we get moved to the hotel."

"Maggie, please, make yourself at home."

Maggie gently caressed Susan's shoulder, then moved to briefly touch Susan's cheek. "Thank you." With that she turned, walked into her room, and started to unpack some items from her overnight bag.

Susan placed her hand on her cheek. She watched as Maggie pulled things from her luggage. Her movements were slow and deliberate. Susan struggled to breathe. Maggie had a definite grace and sensuality. While she didn't meet most people's criteria for classic beauty, she had a magnetism that caused others to notice her. Tall, lean body. Languid movements of a cat, carefully sorting through her possessions.

Finally she held up a midnight blue satin nightshirt with buttons down the front and long tails in the front and back. *Maggie would be stunning in it*, Susan decided. Her breathing became shallow and rapid as she watched. Maggie held the nightshirt, examining it, running her hand up and down the fabric. Susan realized that Maggie knew she was watching yet she refused to acknowledge Susan's presence.

Susan had become a voyeur, unwilling to pull herself away. Maggie removed her blazer, slowly folding it over a chair. Next she slipped off her loafers as she unhooked her leather belt. Only as Maggie unbuttoned her jeans did Susan force herself to turn away.

Susan returned to the kitchen and mechanically attempted to make tea. No cogent thought surfaced—only emotions and images. The water boiled out, forcing her to refill the pot. On the third attempt she was able to force herself to focus on the simple act of making tea. As Maggie walked into the kitchen she was setting two cups of tea on the table. Susan's heart rate had finally returned to normal...until Maggie entered.

Wet hair hanging down below her shoulders, moisture glistening on her face as well as all exposed parts of her body, Maggie was every bit as stunning as Susan had imagined. Susan's reaction was visceral. The desire to touch was more intense than anything she had ever experienced. She curled her hands into tight fists to keep from reaching out. Maggie's nightshirt reached mid-thigh, and well-formed, tanned legs were clearly visible. She was beautiful. *How does she manage it? She either works out or keeps herself physically fit in other ways.*

Maggie's movements were again deliberate and graceful. She walked to the table, pulled out a chair, and sat. One leg folded under her and the other foot resting on the seat with her knee just under her chin, she stared up at Susan.

Susan knew she was in trouble. She turned away with a not-so-gentle reminder to herself that Maggie was a married woman with two children. She also briefly considered that she didn't have time for a relationship, even if Maggie wasn't straight. *Relationship? What am I thinking?* Sometimes reality was better than a cold shower.

"I seem to be constantly thanking you," Maggie said. Her voice was soft, her eyes inviting. That wonderful lopsided smile was just beginning. "I insist you let me make it up some way. I won't take no for an answer."

Susan had to stay focused on the sheer act of picking up the cup to avoid spilling it. "You really don't have to do anything. I know what it's like to be stranded." *Yeah, right! You don't go outside to pick up the paper without a detailed plan for how you open the door, how quickly you walk, how you bend and pick up the paper. Stranded? I am never stranded. Not me!* Even her mother questioned where Susan developed this compulsion to organize every facet of her life.

"I told you. I won't take no. In fact, if you and your family don't have any plans for Thanksgiving, I would like you to be my guests. That's when Derek arrives. I realize you may have other plans, but if not, please say yes."

Susan wanted to say yes, but then she remembered: *Thanksgiving is in two weeks. It's my turn to cook. My sister and her family are coming over.* And then the thorns of reality began to pierce.

"Susan, are you okay?"

"Yes, I…I'm…I'm fine," she muttered.

Oh, shit. Shit! Shit! Shit! What have I done? All her fears and inhibitions attacked at once. *Some evil plot, surely.* Her life had been a constant battle for control. Control made her comfortable but also allowed her to postpone decisions. Especially about her personal life. She felt control slipping. *Oh, shit.*

Chapter Three

Unsure what to do, Maggie placed her empty cup on the table and stood. She tried to remember the last time she had just talked with another woman. *Maybe Derek is right, I need to learn how to have friends. Keep it light*, she reminded herself. *This gracious woman is just being kind.*

She searched for some words to bridge the gap growing between them. Maggie was not one to initiate conversation. Others sought her. She merely had to choose whom to respond to or whom to ignore. Along the way she had lost the art of graceful conversation.

"Look, Susan, if I've said something or done something, I...I..." Maggie struggled. Her emotions were a whirlwind, confusing and treacherous. "I'm sorry. Maybe I should go ahead and get dressed and see if I can have someone pick us up and take us to the hotel." Maggie picked up her cup. "I'm sure we can figure something out." She trailed off as she waited for some response.

When Susan finally turned to face her, Maggie saw the tears gently sliding down the side of Susan's face. A knot tightened around Maggie's heart. She wanted desperately to reach out and wipe away those tears, to hold Susan, to reassure her. Desire and anguish were at war. She did nothing, clenching her teeth. An army of aides and assistants handled every area of her life.

She had not needed to take care of her own problems, much less someone else's.

Susan wiped away the tears. "Maggie, don't leave. It's not you. I'm tired and feeling a little overwhelmed. Besides, you don't have any money or identification, remember? I'd like for you to meet Cady and my mom." She gave Maggie a quick hug. "I'll give you an answer about Thanksgiving later, okay?"

Accustomed to giving orders and having things fixed immediately, Maggie remained uncomfortably silent.

"May I use your phone?" Maggie asked as Susan left the kitchen. "My cell phone is dead and I need to let Derek know we're okay."

"Of course. Sleep well."

Maggie's arms and shoulders ached. She unclenched her hands and tried to relax. For once, neither money nor fame could fix the situation. She mentally replayed the day in fast forward. Only when the familiar male voice answered was she able to relax. "Hi, Derek. It's me."

"Maggie, where are you? Are you okay? Your agent has been calling the hotel and they said you never checked in. We've been worried."

"Derek, we're all safe. How's Paul?"

"He's fine. Worried." Derek was returning to calmer levels. "I'm so glad you are all okay. Are you at the hotel? What happened?"

Maggie tried to frame an answer. No matter what she said, the truth was stranger. In her infatuation with Susan, she had forgotten that a simple call to the hotel or her agent might have prevented any misunderstandings. "Do you want details or the *Reader's Digest* version?"

"Maggie, just tell me what happened."

As if recounting ordinary series of facts, Maggie talked about the late start, the delays, the plane problems, and the missing identification. She ignored any interruptions and rushed into the generous offer from the woman she had met on the plane. There was silence on the other end. She could guess what Derek was thinking, but he was wrong. "Derek, Susan's a good person. She's a successful businesswoman with a child of her own. We're very safe here."

"Maggie, I don't believe this. How could you allow some stranger take you and the kids somewhere?"

"Damn it, Derek, what do you think is going to happen in five to six hours, especially with everyone asleep?" Maggie recognized that in the past she had made stupid mistakes. Stupid mistakes that dearly cost her. *Not now*, she argued, *not now*. "Her mother and daughter are in the house. In the morning, when my wallet arrives, I'll check into the hotel." *Maybe*.

"Maggie, what do you know about this woman? What does she want? Does she know who you are?"

"You're right," Maggie answered, taking the offensive, "I don't know a damn thing about her. She's probably a decent, hardworking single parent, living in a very traditional fucking middle-class neighborhood. And, no, I don't think she has the faintest idea what I do or who the fuck I am. Derek, I could be one of those California crazies and yet she offered to let me and the kids stay here. And she's asked for nothing. *Nothing!* I think she'd have more to worry about from me than I do about from her."

"Hang on, Mags. I'm sorry. I just don't want you hurt. Let Paul run a check on her. She could be another Brenda Harper. Whether she is or she isn't, she'll never know we checked."

Maggie again felt the hurt, anger, and embarrassment. "Derek, she's not Brenda." Even as she spoke, Maggie began to have doubts. Brenda had been Maggie's last relationship, someone Maggie thought she could love, but Brenda had only been interested in Maggie's fame and money, even threatening to out Maggie when things ended between them.

"Mags, let me find out. I can have Paul make some inquiries.

I don't want to see you hurt. What's her name? What else can you tell me about her?" Maggie sighed and gave him what information she knew from the business card they had exchanged earlier.

"Look, she's probably a Girl Scout leader." Maggie tried to lighten the mood. "You have to admit CPAs are not exactly adventurers."

"Maggie, I'm sorry. If something happened to you or the kids, I would be lost. And I don't want to see you hurt again."

Swallowing hard, she recalled the times she had come crying to Derek with a broken heart. That was years ago, and at some point she had given up on love and being hurt, deciding to keep her relationships loose, no entanglements. Light affairs. "Snacks," she had even called them once. No commitments. *Except for Derek and the kids and work. And now Paul.*

"Me either," she whispered into the phone. "Thanks, Bubba. Tell Paul I said hello."

"Please be careful, Mags. I'll give Paul a hug for you."

"Yeah, yeah! When you start hugging, make sure you tell him the first one is from me. Otherwise you'll get too busy to even remember that I called."

Derek laughed. "I'll tell him."

Maggie replaced the phone in the cradle and sat quietly. The silence of the house surrounded her. The kitchen was white, large, and designed for cooking. She admired the clean, organized countertops and the comfortable feel. She smiled when she noticed how the jars and canisters were carefully aligned by height. A counter separated the kitchen from the family room, toys still scattered on the floor. Maggie doubted if that was the way the room looked when Susan was home. A large flat panel screen occupied one wall and a stone fireplace decorated another. She wondered briefly if Susan had a husband or a boyfriend around.

Her own house was landscaped and had live plants everywhere. Although she enjoyed them, she had never cared for them. She and Derek had housekeepers and plant keepers and animal keepers. She realized she lived a well-kept life.

She headed for the bedroom. Even on her last tour, she had been in bed no later than three. *Well*, she reminded herself, *I'm over thirty and on my way to forty. I can't do all the things I did when I was twenty.*

She pulled back the covers and climbed into the daybed. Everything here reminded her of Susan. Organized, thorough, safe. She smiled. There was very little out of place. Much more organized than her own life.

Maggie recalled the look on Susan's face as they moved the files. Initially tentative but then turning warm, sensitive, vibrant.

Faint memories resurrected a time, when she was in college, when she had many women friends and a committed, loving relationship. When was the last time she had been emotionally and physically close with a woman? Not just sex. What had happened? When did it happen? It was so long ago, it seemed more a fragment of another life. The thoughts grew dim and cold.

Maggie turned her thoughts back to Susan and once again began to feel warm. A long-dormant hunger surprised her. Maggie imagined touching Susan, kissing her. She could almost feel Susan's fingers moving across her thighs with such incredible gentleness, she thought she would die with pleasure. It had been too long since she had been touched by another woman, and Susan was damned attractive. With these pleasant thoughts, she fell asleep.

CHAPTER FOUR

Some elusive memory danced at the edges of Susan's consciousness, refusing to loosen sleep's tenuous grip and keeping her in a light sleep. She desperately wanted closure. She hated loose endings and unfinished stories. "Mommy" whispered into her ear brought her fully awake.

"Hi, sunshine." Susan lifted Cady onto the bed. "I missed you, sweetheart." Susan's eyes, ears, and heart flew open. Cady giggled as she cuddled next to Susan.

"Mommy, look!" Cady squirmed upright and pointed to the end of the bed. Susan looked and saw the shy brown eyes and familiar grin of little D.J. as he stood at the foot of the bed. Without a thought, she pulled him onto the bed too.

"Cady, this is D.J. Can you say hello?"

Cady nodded, but made no sound. Susan was touched by this sudden shyness. "Cady Hettinger, can't you say hello to our visitor?" Cady put her arms around Susan's neck and hid her face.

"Where's my mommy?" D.J. asked barely above a whisper.

"She's…" The dream memory was no longer vague or dancing in Susan's head. "She's sleeping. Why don't we go into the kitchen and I'll fix us something to eat." The last thing she wanted to do was cook, but she needed to deal with the night's events and entertain two children. Since Cady enjoycd being a helper, she gladly took D.J.'s hand and led him to the other side of the house. Susan quickly changed into a pair of shorts and a T-shirt, carefully folding her sleepwear, then she headed toward the kitchen.

The smell of coffee emanating from the direction of the kitchen told Susan that her mother was already awake. Her mom, an early riser, loved to put the coffee on and sit in the kitchen or, on nice mornings, on the patio, and read the paper. *Oh, dear goddess*, Susan prayed, struggling for an explanation for strangers in the house, *let this be a gorgeous morning*. She needed a few more minutes to come up with a logical explanation. *Logical! Last night I didn't want anything to do with logic*. As soon as she walked into the kitchen, Susan knew this was not a day for celebrating answered prayers.

"Hi, Mom," Susan said a little too cheerfully. As she hugged her mother, she glanced briefly at the kitchen clock. It was only 7:30 a.m. No wonder her mind felt like a bad case of furballs.

Her mother smiled at her, put her paper down, and rose to get another coffee cup. "Good morning. How was your trip? What time did you get in?"

Before she could answer, three little urchins raced across the kitchen into the family room and promptly turned on the electronic babysitter. Susan turned to her mom. She sat quietly for such a long time that Susan almost had hope that this would be a normal morning.

Her mother Maureen was very Irish. With her fiery red hair now dominated by streaks of gray, she still looked like a leprechaun, waiting for some joke or jest to take place. This was one of those times.

"Oh, dear," her mom muttered, "I guess I'll need more orange juice." As her mom walked to the refrigerator, Susan just watched, wondering what was going on. The more direct inquiry, the gentle nagging, even the motherly meddling she was familiar with, but not this. Three children were sitting noisily watching TV and her mother was at the sink pouring more juice.

Okay, I can do this, Susan thought. *We'll pretend strange children are often here and then I won't have to explain.* She walked up to the stove and got out the large frying pan.

"Susan, why don't you go jump into the shower," she said, "and I'll get this started? Shall I fix bacon first?"

Her mother looked sane but that wasn't a consoling thought. Maureen was unpredictable and observant. Actually, "nosy" would be a better word. Today she seemed more like a Stepford mother, acting as if this were routine. Susan feared some type of derangement had descended upon her entire family. "That's okay. I'll do it," she said in her best nonchalant, assertive voice. Not a single question had been asked. True, these were miniature strangers, but surely there must be some full-grown person to whom they belonged. Either that or Susan had resorted to kidnapping.

"No, dear, you go run take a shower and I'll get this started."

Susan looked carefully at her mother, trying to read any hint from her face. *Nothing.*

"Thanks, Mom. I'll hurry."

In her bedroom, Susan gathered clean clothes—another pair of shorts and a shirt that matched—neatly folded her dirty clothes, and put them in the clothes hamper. Less than five minutes later she was back in the kitchen.

"Beth, will you turn down the TV, and I want all three of you to come sit at the table." Her mom had already learned their names. Susan felt her control slipping. Her stomach chose to announce its presence with a loud rumble. "Dear, are you hungry?" Her mother looked at her and then at the offending body part.

"A little," Susan barely squeaked out. She looked at the kitchen scene. From the children's dress, it was obvious they'd spent the night. *Why isn't she asking questions?* There had been times throughout Susan's life when it seemed the whole world would be falling apart and her mom wouldn't notice or would simply say "how nice, dear." Other times she would not so subtly ask a variety of questions until she got the desired answers. Susan's father often said it was because her mother was Irish and all Irish believed in wee people and magic. If something was illogical, it was magic. That rarely helped Susan to understand, or be like, her mother.

What has she learned from them while I was in the shower? Susan wondered. Her internal voices argued. After all, what could they have said? You met on a plane and you're letting them and their mommy sleep here. Another voice yelled, "Oh, God!" Susan sat at the table unable to handle any further arguing.

"Susan, will you make more coffee? I guess we'll need a full pot."

"Of course, Mom." Susan got up and mechanically made coffee. *I've got to say something.* "Mom, I, uh, we have company."

"Yes, dear."

"I mean, Maggie, the children's mother, was stranded at the airport."

Maureen stopped cooking and stared at Susan. "Dear, are you trying to tell me you brought a friend home?"

"Well, I…" Susan stumbled for some plausible explanation. "I, uh, didn't know until the last minute. I mean, it was a late decision." Very late.

"Yes, Susan's a godsend." Maggie's entrance was perfectly timed. She glanced at Susan with that half grin and a twinkle in her eyes. She wore a pair of white shorts that framed her beautiful legs and a white Hard Rock Café London T-shirt that left little for speculation.

Susan was speechless and just stared. "What? Uh?"

Maureen stuck out her hand. "I'm Susan's mom, Maureen. I've already met your kids."

"Margaret Carson-Baxter, and I'm delighted to meet you. Please call me Maggie. Susan told me so much about you."

"Well, I must admit this is the first time Susan has brought home a girlfriend that actually spent the night. I don't know much about you yet, but I am sure I will, and quickly." Maureen grabbed Maggie and hugged her as if they two were old friends.

Susan quickly leaned against the nearest wall, realizing the morning had quickly become her worst nightmare. No one spoke, only the soft drone of the television accompanied this melodrama. *What are all these strange people doing in my kitchen? Where is my quiet, serene Saturday?* Silently, Susan made a list of all the things she would willingly give up if she could just find herself back in bed and dreaming.

Maggie looked briefly at her and then at her mom. "Maureen, I can tell that you and I will get along fine." She turned toward the stove. "Whatever you're cooking smells wonderful. Can I help?"

"Nonsense, you go sit with Susan and the kids. Susan will join you as soon as she recovers from her bad manners. Honestly, Susan, you should find out what Maggie wants in her coffee. Make her feel welcome." Maureen turned again to Maggie. "My daughter doesn't date much, but that's no excuse for her manners."

Maggie hugged all three children and sat at the table. She smiled at Susan and patted the seat next to her. "Come sit down, honey."

Panic filled Susan. She had been outed in her own house. She reached for her orange juice and wished it had vodka in it. *What is Maggie thinking? Will she grab her kids and run?*

Maggie instead smiled and asked for coffee. Susan's mom moved the food quickly to the table and soon they were chatting as if they had known each other for a long time. As she looked around the table, Susan remembered her mother taking her to see the play *Peter Pan*. She always got excited during the part where the audience was asked to bring Tinker Bell back to life. If she died, there would no longer be any magic and Never Land would disappear.

Susan had to save Tink and Peter and Wendy and every child's dream. I *do* believe in fairies, I *do* believe in fairies.

Maybe if she said something enough times, she could wish it to be true. Here she was sitting next to Maggie, her children, her own daughter, and her mother, all sitting at the table as if they belonged together. She liked the feeling.

She watched Maggie's hands as she entertained her mother with tales of their travels yesterday. They were all laughing and enjoying the conversation. What was this woman's secret?

CHAPTER FIVE

Maggie's mind was traveling at hyperspeed. Meeting Susan's mother had been interesting but discovering the information about her host was more important. Susan was a lesbian! Savoring the thought, she lifted the coffee cup to her lips, hiding the grin she knew was spreading across her face. Like a fine brandy, she tasted the thought, just a small sip, and let it roll around until she was able to savor the full flavor.

"Maggie?" Maureen interrupted. "Maggie, are you okay?" After breakfast, Susan had gone to her office to work on reports. Maureen and Maggie had remained chatting in the kitchen after breakfast.

"I'm sorry," Maggie said. "Did you say something?"

"My daughter is very good at what she does, but in personal relationships she will do just about anything to avoid hurting another person's feelings." Maureen hesitated. "I hope it doesn't bother you that my daughter is gay."

Maggie nearly choked on her coffee. Both women quickly grabbed napkins and cleaned up the spill from the cup Maggie hastily put down. "No, no, that's okay." She tried to sound calm in spite of a racing pulse.

"I wish Susan could find a nice person, someone like you," Maureen continued.

What? Maggie was startled by Susan's mother. *So do I, Maureen. But now what do I say?*

"I don't mean to offend you. I love my daughter unconditionally. When Susan first told me she was gay, I didn't really understand. I guess most parents feel that way. Susan is so traditional and rigid. I was almost relieved to think she was doing something so unexpected." Maureen laughed at her own joke. "I'm sorry. She really struggled with all this and I am proud of her for the person she is today." Maureen paused. "She dated a woman, a real nice woman, for six months, but they never lived together. It didn't work out. Then two years later, she surprised me and married Cady's father. That lasted about a year. He left when Susan became pregnant. There really hasn't been anyone serious since."

Maggie was glad her coffee cup was empty. She didn't know what to say to Susan's mother. She only knew that she had met an attractive woman she genuinely liked.

"I'm glad you like her," Maureen replied. "And I think she is a good-looking woman too, but she is my daughter."

Flushing with embarrassment, Maggie realized she had been thinking out loud. "Susan is a wonderful, easy-to-like person. I rarely meet many sincere people in my work. As a result, I don't have a lot of friends. You and Susan have been wonderful to me and my family, and I'm not likely to forget that."

A self-satisfied grin spread easily across Maureen's face. "Good," she said. "And how long will you be in Orlando? You will stay with us."

A good-looking woman and a mother who wanted to play matchmaker. *Hot damn.* Maggie was charmed. "Thank you. If you really mean it, I would love to stay. As long as I won't intrude on you or Susan…"

"Nonsense. If Susan brought you and your kids here, she must want you to be here." With that, Maureen went outside to check on the kids.

Once Maggie was alone, her thoughts returned to her

host. Susan's strength and serenity. The feeling of being safe with her. Then she hastily added, *and her family.* Only Derek had ever offered that kind of safety. As she sat in the kitchen, she imagined what it would be like to live there. It didn't take long for conjecture to lead to arousal. Thoughts of her own life interrupted and she reined in her emotions. *Derek may be right. My life is just beginning to have some semblance of order.* She pulled out her now fully charged cell phone and called home.

When Paul answered, Maggie greeted him warmly. After a few brief exchanges, Paul asked, "Maggie, what's going on?"

There was nothing challenging or threatening, just a warm, friendly greeting. Paul was a friend, their attorney, and Derek's lover. "Paul, everything I said last night is true. Susan's been great and her mother is a real trip." Maggie proceeded to give him details, including Maureen's invitation to stay, carefully leaving out her emotional responses to Susan. "I like Susan and want to get to know her. You can be persuasive. Talk to Derek.

"I'll talk to him, but, please be careful."

"I will. Thanks."

❖

The next day, Susan proposed a cookout. Susan and Maggie headed for the grocery store to round up a few supplies while her mother and the kids prepared the remainder of the meal.

The shopping trip was a cultural experience for Maggie. During the fifteen-minute drive to the store, they traveled tree-lined streets with well-kept green lawns. Children rode bicycles and occasionally an adult could be seen at work in the yard. Lawn mowers raced back and forth, trimming the grass lawns. Winter plants provided an array of color.

At the grocery store, Maggie realized she hadn't shopped for much of anything in the last ten years. She followed Susan up and down aisles, staring at lights, at people, and at brightly colored packages designed to lure the impulsive shopper. Susan, at times mistaking Maggie's staring for interest, would throw an item into the basket and steer to the next stop. When they reached the counter they realized they had a basket full of groceries, sans the items they originally set out to purchase. "Oops," Maggie said, "I guess we forgot something."

Laughing, Susan agreed. "But this time we stick to the list. My mother will shoot us both if we add any more." They laughed and once again made a quick, but more purposeful, tour of the aisles.

Back at home, Susan's controlling self took over and she was soon a field general directing her troops, moving food and organizing the cooking.

Watching this organized efficiency, Maggie was amused. The more she watched, the more attracted she became to Susan. Susan moved with more purpose and efficiency as the meal preparations progressed. Occasionally, Maggie would catch Susan looking at her. She loved the way Susan turned red when caught staring. Susan had a wholesome "girl next door" look. Her honey blond hair, pulled back into a simple ponytail, glowed in the Florida sun. Her eyes, now shaded with sunglasses, were almost the same shade as her hair, but flecked with green like a summer day and almost as warm. Maggie was glad her own sunglasses prevented Susan from noticing the care with which she was examining her well-shaped form—or the effect Susan's smile was having on her. She was willing to bet Susan was unaware of just how attractive she was or the effect she could have on others. *Maybe that's part of the attraction.*

"Are you sure there isn't anything I can do?" Maggie asked.

Susan smiled and shook her head. "You're still company. Next time you wash dishes."

Susan's smile was dazzling. Maggie's heart lurched. They both laughed.

Lunch was ready and Maggie disposed of her now empty bottle of beer and grabbed a couple of paper plates, quickly fixing the kids' food and watching them eat. The enthusiasm her own children showed in emptying their plates amazed her. She filled her plate and sat back in a chair to eat and enjoy the conversation. She couldn't remember the last time she had been this relaxed.

After he finished eating, D.J. crawled into her lap. Soon Beth joined him and Maggie was happy. A few minutes later Cady came over and stood quietly looking. Maggie smiled, patted her lap, and made room for her. *Yes, this is definitely peaceful*, she thought as she leaned her chin on Beth's head. She closed her eyes, allowing the good feeling. She heard Susan and her mother talking as they cleaned up but could barely understand either woman. The Florida sun warmed her and she allowed her body to truly relax.

"Hey, sleepyhead." Susan's voice startled her. Maggie couldn't remember falling asleep. *That's a first. Most nights I have trouble falling asleep.*

"Come on, let's get the kids inside," Susan said.

Maggie helped her children brush their teeth and then stayed with them until they fell asleep. Cady had fallen asleep quickly. Before leaving the room, she looked at the sleeping children, realizing how comfortable this all felt. *It would be so easy. Easy for what?* The answer scared her.

As Maggie walked into the kitchen, Susan was just beginning to wash the dishes.

"So, am I still a guest or do I roll up my sleeves?"

"There's not much to wash, but you can put away the cold stuff. Thanks."

"You're welcome." Maggie smiled. "I don't remember the last time I've…" *I've what? Felt relaxed, safe, cared for.* These feelings disturbed Maggie and she searched for an answer. "I've had such a wonderful time."

"I didn't do anything special. Just a family weekend."

"My family never cooked out," Maggie said. "In fact, we rarely did anything as a family. It's a word I don't use when I think of my past. Unfortunately, Derek and I are always so busy we don't usually do things like this." *We have cooks and staff,* she reminded herself.

Susan sensed there was much more being unsaid. "Then I'm glad you're here enjoying my family. And now you're a part of it, so get busy." Maggie's laughter warmed her and a barrier was lowered.

"I really like your mother and your family. It's so different from my own family growing up," Maggie said.

"I'm lucky, and I know it. My mom and dad have always been so supportive. Dad was traditional, organized, quiet, shy. I guess more like me. And Mom is opinionated, impulsive, and outspoken. I never knew what she was going to say or do." Maggie nodded. "Dad died four months after Cady was born. He was just as excited about her as he was his first grandchild. I really miss him." She turned back to the sink, finishing off the last of the dishes, carefully loading the dishwasher. "At first I was panicked when I became pregnant. Being a single parent scared the stew out of me and wasn't in my plan. Maybe that was part of the problem. I was struggling with my sexuality, my career, and being pregnant, all at the same time. I hate it when things are not organized and sorted out." Susan smiled. "Somehow I survived."

"I've always wanted children," Maggie said. "I wanted a house, pets—the whole thing. Derek wanted to wait until we were settled. For a while, I was afraid we'd never have kids. Now my life with them is a shelter. I don't know what I'd do if anything happened to them. Maybe that's why I'm so protective. That and the fact that I want to do a better job than my own parents." Realizing she had revealed too much, Maggie quickly changed the subject to safer topics. She talked of working through college and all-night study sessions. "I supported myself all through college. I wonder now how I survived on three to four hours a night. That and canned soup."

Susan nodded. "My sister used to take me out for dinner

MAGIC OF THE HEART

twice a week. She was sure I would study my way through school and never meet anyone and probably starve."

"My mother died at thirty-six from cancer because we couldn't afford doctors," Maggie said. "After that, my family gradually fell apart. We just didn't have much keeping us together. I worry sometimes that I give my kids too much, but I don't want them to struggle the way I did."

"It's hard to have balance as to when something is too much," Susan said.

As Susan closed the dishwasher, she turned and found Maggie less than a foot away. Her pulse quickened and heat began at her throat, quickly moving up her face. They stood staring at each other for what seemed an eternity.

Maggie's eyes traveled down to Susan's lips. *They need to be kissed*, Maggie thought. *I need to be kissed*, she silently amended. She moved closer to see if Susan would pull away. Nothing happened. Maggie saw an echo of her own hunger in Susan's eyes. Maggie could only think about the softness of Susan's lips. How they would feel, how they would taste. *I need to move slowly*, she reminded herself. The tension between them increased until it seemed like there was an audible pounding matching the beating of their own hearts.

The doorbell rang twice before either recognized the sound. Maggie pulled away first, making some mental comment about timing. When Susan returned, she handed a package to Maggie containing the well-traveled wallet.

"Hurray for honesty." Susan tried to lighten the moment.

Maggie stared at the leather Gucci wallet, turning it over and over in her hand. Susan's comment made her feel uneasy. Finally looking up, she said, "I want to thank you for allowing us to enjoy your bed-and-breakfast, but I probably should rent a car and move my family to the hotel tonight."

Susan's heart pounded in her chest as she struggled to take a deep breath. That was nothing compared to the painful throbbing in the pit of her stomach. She watched Maggie lift and examine each item in the wallet and then replace it.

Good, Susan, your pulse is now down to a thousand beats per minute.

Maggie sat with her long, tanned legs folded under, seeming at ease within her own body. After two years in therapy, Susan was still self-conscious and inhibited. Except around Maggie. Her pulse rate was accelerating again. Maggie looked up at her, lips curving into that now familiar half-smile. Lips Susan nearly kissed.

Susan's emotions took off again, racing like some Grand Prix of feelings. What was it about Maggie? She felt possessed... or obsessed. She ached to touch those hands. The throbbing Susan felt earlier returned and was now accompanied by a warm wetness. The raceway of emotions came to a screeching halt as Maggie's words sank in.

On impulse Susan said, "Please stay...as long as you like, that is."

Maggie walked over to Susan. She was close enough for Susan to feel warm breath on her cheek. Susan still wanted to kiss her.

"Susan," Maggie spoke softly, forcing Susan to lean closer. "I don't want to intrude. You are a very generous person." She lightly brushed Susan's cheek, gliding her fingers slowly into soft golden hair. Maggie took a deep breath and lowered her hand. "I don't think you would ask me to leave even if you wanted me to. I assure you we can afford to stay anywhere we want."

"I want you..." The words were out and never passed through any gray matter for filtering. Susan hesitated, realizing she was in trouble. "To stay."

Susan imagined hearing Maggie's breathing. Maybe it was just her own lungs struggling to find the right mixture of chemicals to clear the cobwebs from her shrouded brain.

"Susan, you are amazing." Maggie leaned forward only inches, but enough to softly and briefly kiss Susan.

Her lips were like warm snowflakes. Only there briefly. Susan leaned in to claim more than a brief touch.

"My, you are persuasive." Maggie laughed.

Panicked by her own behavior, Susan pulled away. "Maggie, I'm sorry. I didn't mean for that to happen. Please forgive me. I'm not trying to make a pass. I've never done anything like that before. I am so sorry."

Maggie placed her fingers on Susan's lips, silencing them. "Don't apologize. Come on, it's really okay, and I started it. We're both adults. Let's get the kids up."

Susan stood numb and watched Maggie walk toward the back of the house. Her imagination kicked into overdrive. *If I'm not crazy, then the rest of the world is. Oh, shit!* She reviewed all the food and beverages consumed in the last twenty-four hours, hoping some rare form of food poisoning caused her strange behavior. Not finding any consolation, or logic, in her diet, she decided work would occupy her mind until control took over. She headed for the kitchen, called her mother, and began cleaning the now spotless counters. She quickly sat and put her head down on the table.

"Susan, what's the matter?" Her mother stood over her.

"Mom, I'm okay. I think I'm just a little tired." If her diet had not been the problem, then Susan grasped at sleep deprivation. Eventually, she felt more in control.

The kitchen again filled with laughter and chatter. Watching Maggie, her kids, Cady, and her mom, Susan felt complete.

On Monday, after Susan left for work, Maureen, Maggie, and the three children played tourists around central Florida. First they visited Sea World. "I love watching the whales and the dolphins best of all," Maureen said. "I know most people head out to Disney or Universal Studios. I prefer the water."

"Sea World it is," Maggie said as she herded the kids into

the waiting minivan. Susan had driven her mother's Chrysler New Yorker into work, leaving the larger vehicle behind. "You direct and I'll drive." At that hour there were no long lines. Maggie, dressed in jeans and a Florida State University T-shirt she borrowed from Susan, twice was asked for an autograph.

Maggie readily agreed but added, "I'm here with my family and we'd like to enjoy today uninterrupted. No pictures, please." Maggie caught Maureen staring but she didn't ask any questions.

As they continued to wander around, a large group of teenagers began to follow Maggie. Soon a small crowd had gathered, pressing closer to the group. Concerned about the continued safety of the children, Maggie was apologetic but again requested to be left alone. "I'm sorry. Would you mind if we left?"

Maureen shook her head. "Are there any police looking for you?"

Maggie laughed. "I hope not. At least not yet. Why?"

"I wanted to make sure you weren't wanted for some crime. I don't want Susan getting in trouble."

"Neither do I, Maureen. Neither do I. I just thought it might be a good time to leave, before the traffic picks up." Placing her body between the crowd and the children, Maggie moved toward the exit.

Soon they were on the road headed for home. "I hope I didn't ruin your day, with our leaving early," Maggie said.

"Nonsense," Maureen said. "I get to go here whenever I want. I hope you had a good time. Especially with the interruptions."

Maggie knew Susan's mother was fishing for information. In spite of the welcome Susan and her family had provided, she was not yet ready to reveal too much personal information.

That evening, Sea World was the main topic of conversation. "Thank you for taking my family," Susan said. "Let me reimburse you for their tickets."

"Nonsense. The tickets weren't as expensive as a hotel room." Maggie was adamant. "How was work?"

"Typical Monday. I honestly think film executives spend weekends creating crises and spending money."

Maggie was suddenly much more alert. *Films? I thought she was an accountant.*

"We're backing a film project a group of students from the University of Central Florida are creating. Apparently, one of the students crawled up a tree to shoot a scene." She looked at Maggie. "Well, guess what? All that weight, and the kid and camera fell out of the tree." Interpreting the look on Maggie's face as concern, she explained. "The student ended up in the hospital. He's okay but the camera is in pieces. The university is afraid the kid's family will sue, and now they're short a production camera. Since we provided the financial backing, UCF's attorney called us to check on our liability."

Maggie tried to remain calm. "You're involved with filmmaking?"

"I'm not. My company finances a variety of media projects. I review, audit, and negotiate. My boss usually does most of the up-front work, especially the big projects. I'm just the bean counter that keeps everyone under budget."

"You don't look like a bean counter," Maggie said. "Do you work with just independent productions? Is that what you do? Work in the entertainment field?"

"My boss Ed worked in California with the film industry. He was put in charge of an office in Florida when Disney opened and then he decided to go on his own. Ed persuaded me to come to work for him. Now I'm his CFO."

Stretching her legs out, Susan changed her position on the couch so that she could see Maggie easier. "I don't know why he picked me. He laughs and teases me about my complete ignorance of most entertainers."

"You must be really good at what you do, then."

"I'm organized and driven. Ed is not. He's the people pleaser. I'm the people killer."

Maggie relaxed. "And you definitely are organized. Why are you called the people killer?"

Susan was pleased that Maggie hadn't looked bored during their discussion and hadn't yet said "how nice." "Because I've got to tell people they can't get everything they want, or that money was spent inappropriately. Most of the time it ends up in arguing."

"And who wins?"

"The person who controls the purse."

❖

While Maggie, her mother, and the kids enjoyed the week, Susan struggled at work. By Thursday, she'd had enough. "Damn it, Bruce, there is nothing in the proposal or contract that allows any member of the filming crew to climb a tree. I've talked to our lawyers and they're behind us. Tell the family we'll see them in court."

Bruce Ringer, a local attorney representing the student's family, urged Susan to reconsider. "It will be a lot less expensive to settle out of court."

"Bruce, the answer is no. We'll have P.I.'s checking every activity this kid was involved in. It's your choice."

"Damn you, Susan, you're—"

"Sorry, gotta run. If you have any other questions, speak to our attorneys." She hung up. "What a pain."

Susan looked at the computer in front of her. "I've had enough for today." She shut it down and headed for home. She was enjoying having Maggie and the kids around.

By Saturday, Susan was ready for non-work time. Her mother suggested a visit to Church Street Station, the downtown Orlando attraction. Maggie was as curious and noisy as the kids, quickly moving from one shop to another, picking up and trying various gifts, toys, and unusual objects.

"Let's go to the Mercantile, Susan. They can play some games and we can all get something to eat," her mother said.

Maggie immediately wandered over to the game area. "I like this one," Susan said pointing to an arcade game nearby. "It's called Bop the Gator. That's an appropriate activity for an FSU grad."

A questioning expression and a head tilt was Maggie's response.

"Florida State and the University of Florida are rivals. Florida's mascot is an alligator."

"Ah, so you liked smashing the gator with that toy hammer." Maggie grinned. "Want to try? How about a little one-on-one?"

A small crowd began to surround the loud group. A pulsing light from a camera drew Maggie's immediate attention and she turned away before the camera snapped. "Come on, let's go," Maggie said, grabbing her children by their hands.

"What's wrong?" Susan asked.

"I'm tired. Let's go home."

❖

Maggie paced the family room as she waited for Susan to return from running a few errands after their aborted afternoon outing. After nine years she still had the urge to smoke. Instead, she sipped her wine and tried to sort through her feelings. She had no doubts about the attraction to Susan. After all, it had been years since she had been sexually involved with anyone.

These new feelings, however, were unsettling. *Keep things light. Have fun, move on. Maybe I'm just horny.* The sweet gentleness of Susan's lips. The music in her laughter. The warmth in her voice. Holding the glass up to the light, she watched as sweat formed on the outside of the glass and slowly began to run down the sides. She stroked the sides of the glass. *Learn to be a friend*, she told herself. *It could be a good experience.* She put the glass down.

The garage door opening stopped further ruminations. Maggie sat on the couch and pretended to read.

From the look on Susan's face, Maggie could tell that something was bothering her, and she wasn't sure she wanted to know what it was. For one brief moment she wondered if Susan could read her mind.

"I didn't realize you were interested in financial management."

Maggie blushed, realizing she had picked up one of Susan's professional journals. No wonder the thing was so damn boring. Chagrined, she replied, "Actually, I was looking for any prurient pictures."

"It might help if you turned the magazine upright." Susan laughed and joined Maggie on the couch. They sat for a few moments, enjoying the quiet. Finally, Susan turned and faced Maggie. "I need to offer some apologies"—she paused to gather courage—"and some explanations."

Maggie sat back and decided to, for once, be quiet.

"I'm not ashamed of being a lesbian. I've had such mixed feelings about sexuality…about sex, period. There are some things that I'm just slow at. I see twenty-year-olds who are so confident and proud. I wasn't, but I'm getting there."

Susan stopped, poured herself a glass of wine, and took a sip to regain her faltering courage. "When I…when I…" She took another sip and continued. "When I kissed you, I was out of line. I've never done anything like that. I'm not sure…" Susan could no longer look at Maggie. She focused instead on the glass of wine in her hands. "All evening, actually all week, I was afraid that you were going to just pick up and leave. I'm sorry. I'd understand if you do want to leave. I'll even drive you wherever you wanted to go. I promise nothing will happen. I promise."

Tears filled the corner of Susan's eyes. Maggie was torn

between the desire to trust and the need to protect herself. She took Susan's hand. "You don't need to apologize. If I felt uncomfortable with you, I would have told you. But I don't." The next words were more difficult. Realizing that Susan was becoming important to her, she wanted to take a risk, yet years of self-preservation had taught the lesson of caution well. "As for our kissing, Susan, I..." Now Maggie had to choose her words carefully. "I...I think I wanted that kiss. I do want us to be friends."

Susan reached for Maggie's hand. "Thank you. I've been driving myself crazy. I do that sometimes. My mom tells me I need to think more positively." Susan paused, gathering courage. "I'm not very good at personal relationships. I've never had very many friends, much less..." She hesitated. She had never talked about anything this personal with anyone other than her sister. "I don't have a lot of experience with romantic relationships." She laughed at her comment, "I have little or no experience. One failed marriage and one failed lesbian relationship. Guess I'm still in the novice category." Susan felt her face turn red.

Maggie grabbed Susan's hand with both of hers. "I've never been good with any kind of relationships, whether work, social, or personal. Derek has been my only friend for as long as I can remember." Maggie swallowed hard as she realized she was on unfamiliar ground. "I know this. Right now, more than anything, I want to get to know you better. I'm not very good at this kind of thing, so I may make some mistakes."

Already Maggie knew the road ahead was littered with complications. She wasn't even sure she knew what she expected from Susan, or what Susan was willing to give. She just knew Susan was different. Susan liked her as Maggie, human being, not rock star, not wealthy woman, just Maggie. That would have to do for now. "I'm enjoying this time. And I'm looking forward to Thanksgiving dinner. Your mom tells me you're a good cook."

Susan laughed. For the remainder of the evening, they held hands and talked.

CHAPTER SIX

The radio alarm going off ended a deep, trouble-free sleep for Susan, the first in almost a week. Thanksgiving dinner was on the agenda, but for a few minutes more, Susan wanted to enjoy the peace. Ed, her boss, had driven her crazy all week looking for some rock star.

"Susan, this could be big. I hear she's looking for financing."

"Who? Why are you asking me?"

"Because I always ask you. M.J. Carson and Reckless. Rumor has it she's trying to save her marriage and is here to dry out. All I need is a list of people or places. How about it?" Susan half listened. With his persistence, and contacts, he was usually successful. When he met a roadblock, he tended to involve Susan and the rest of the staff.

"Look, Ed, if I get you the list of rehab places, will you leave me alone?" He nodded and left but she knew that was not the end of this hunt. While these schemes usually drove her crazy, she knew it didn't compare to the personal chaos in her life.

Susan stretched and thought about the day ahead. Whenever Maggie was around, her emotions and behavior were erratic and out of control. Whether alone or in crowds, Susan was thinking about her, of what she was doing, to whom she was speaking. Maggie was becoming a compulsion, one Susan had no experience dealing with. A given in her life was to never get involved with a woman, much less a married one. Now she was obsessing about a straight, married woman. She headed for a quick shower, trying to focus on Thanksgiving dinner.

The morning was quiet while Susan and her mother fixed the turkey, put it in the oven, and began breakfast. In quick succession, Maggie and all three kids appeared in the kitchen. Susan's life was full.

The quiet ended around eleven when Susan's older sister, Betsy, her husband, Tom, and their three children arrived. Quick introductions were followed by brief awkwardness, then five of the six children ran screaming to Cady's room.

Kyle, the twelve-year-old nephew, followed their exit. "Children," he quietly muttered as he walked toward the family room.

Betsy grinned as Kyle left the kitchen. "My consolation is that one day, I hope, he and his brother and sister will be good friends. After all, we are. So, when do I get to meet this woman who has charmed her way into your house? Mom says she is quite persuasive, at least with you," Betsy teased.

Unnerved by the comment, Susan quickly led them into the kitchen, where they were greeted by the sight of her mother attempting to teach Maggie to make biscuits. Flour covered Maggie's hands and arms. A white smear decorated her left cheek. Her hair, pulled back into a French braid, was streaked with a fine white dust.

"Maggie, I want you to meet my sister and her husband." Susan tried not to giggle. "I'm sorry. You look so funny with flour all over you."

The grin on Susan's face was all that was needed. Maggie grabbed flour with one hand and Susan with her other, smearing flour over Susan's face. Betsy and Tom laughed at them and soon they were targets themselves.

A flour fight would have ensued except for the sound of Kyle interrupting. "Mom! Dad! How gross!" He stood with his hands on his hips trying to look disapproving. Susan tried to laugh but she realized she was probably much like him when she was younger.

❖

Betsy grabbed Maggie and led her to the restroom. "Come on, you have flour all over you. Let's get you cleaned up. Susan is so compulsive, she can care for herself. I figured we could get to know each other without my sister around. She said you met on the plane, but didn't tell me much else. What kind of work do you do?"

Maggie shared the abbreviated version of her life. She had met her husband eighteen years ago while they were in college and, in their senior year, they had gotten married. "Derek plays professional football. This time of year he's often gone. So I decided to take the kids and come to Florida. Susan rescued us when I couldn't rent a car. She's been a lifesaver. We'd probably still be washing dishes and sleeping at the airport if it weren't for her."

Betsy stood quietly with her arms crossed against her chest. "My sister is smart and talented when it comes to work, but she is also trusting and somewhat gullible when it comes to people. She wants to believe most people have good intentions. She wouldn't have allowed you to be here unless she trusts you." Betsy relaxed and stuck out her right hand. "I guess I will too until I learn differently."

Maggie was quite aware of the grilling and its purpose. It was not the first time she had been the subject of such an inquisition, but fame had its way of limiting accessibility. When necessary, she had been able to use humor and charisma to quickly put someone at ease. Today, she was the one who felt uncomfortable. She liked Susan and her family, and the continued verbal dancing was making her uncomfortable.

Maggie recalled Maureen and Cady accompanying her last

week when she had finally checked into the hotel. Maureen clearly noticed the VIP treatment and the large suite they were staying in, but she didn't ask any questions, saying only, "Maggie, I like you, but there are some things about you I don't understand. Something isn't quite right."

Now she was again being grilled by another family member with another promise to respect Susan. She was not comfortable with these feelings or the half-truths she was telling. Life was getting complicated.

"Your sister is one of the nicest people I've ever met. I assure you I respect that." She shook Betsy's hand and they walked back to the kitchen—wary but with a temporary truce.

Tom remained in the kitchen until Kyle reminded him the Dallas Cowboys game was beginning. Maggie also joined them in front of the TV, explaining that her husband would be doing some commentary during the game. Tom asked for his name. Immediately he recognized Derek Baxter. "God, he's a great defensive back."

Maggie sat quietly wondering how much Tom knew. "He's been playing professionally for fourteen years. Eventually he would like to try some other things, but that decision will wait until the end of the season." *Stick to the official media line,* she decided.

"I can't believe this. I'm having dinner with Derek Baxter's wife. No one will believe me. Can you get an autographed picture for me?"

"Sure. When he visits we can even get a picture of the two of you."

"Me too?" Kyle asked.

"You too," Maggie said. No questions about her had yet arisen. She was beginning to feel safer. All further conversation was stopped by introduction of the game commentary staff.

"Betsy, Susan, Mom, come in here. Maggie's husband is going to be on TV." They quietly joined the group around the TV.

❖

Seeing the attractive male talking into the camera was an unsettling reality for Susan. *So, this is the mysterious husband. Not only is he attractive, but he can string multisyllabic words together into intelligent sentences. And he's cocky. Look at him. Susan, I can't believe you. You're acting like a jealous woman. Why? Because everyone is oohing and ahhing over him. So what? Well, at least, I don't have to watch.*

Susan marched back into the kitchen and began to clean up. *Damn, I can't believe I'm this upset over some stupid jock. That jock, in case you have forgotten, is Maggie's husband! Just get control, Susan. Do something useful.* The sponge in her hand became a lot more interesting. She had forgotten how often she used work, any work, to ignore her emotional life.

She was so engrossed in cleaning that she didn't notice someone walk up behind her until she felt Maggie's hand close over hers and stop the scrubbing. "Susan." The whispered voice caused Susan to take a deep breath. "Please look at me."

Maggie's hand remained firmly on Susan's. She closed the distance between them. If Susan turned, she would be in Maggie's arms. "I need to talk to you." She took Susan's hand and led her to the other end of the house where it was quiet.

Closing the door, Maggie asked, "What's the matter?"

Susan tried to leave, but Maggie's hand blocked her exit. She pulled away, but Maggie moved closer. Susan was held a willing captive by dark, penetrating eyes. She found herself incapable of thinking or reasoning. She felt only an unrelenting hunger to touch, to taste, to feel.

Maggie leaned against Susan, shivering with the full body contact. She stroked Susan's hair and gently touched her face. She slowly trailed her fingertips across each brow, carefully studying their shape and texture. She wiped away a tear that had formed in one eye and then tenderly kissed each eyelid. She caressed

Susan's cheek while her fingers danced along the jaw until they stopped at the lips.

Maggie was beyond logical explanations and quick humor. All she could think about was Susan. All she wanted was Susan. Susan's warm breath, Susan's tongue meeting hers.

Susan tried to move away. "I can't. Please let go." Maggie heard the words, but all she could think about was how well their bodies seemed to fit together and how soft Susan's body was. She could not remember such intense desire. She had gone beyond even her own set boundaries, yet she couldn't stop herself. Nor did she want to.

"Susan, oh, God, I want you." Maggie began to kiss her way down Susan's neck. She felt Susan shudder.

"Please!" Maggie felt Susan resisting. "You're married!"

Maggie pulled back. "Susan, there are a lot of things you don't know that I need to explain. Don't judge me, please, not yet. Things aren't the way they seem. I've wanted to tell you, but—"

"Don't, Maggie. You're married." Susan was firm, more in control. "That's all that matters. Please let go."

Maggie knew she had to say something, but what? Years of lies and never having to justify herself had not prepared her for this moment. "Please, Susan, give me a chance to explain." Tears threatened. "I know you don't know much about me. There are so many things going on right now. Just give me a chance. I promise to behave, but let's talk. I…" Maggie struggled with her own emotions. "It's been so long since I've felt this way, and I don't want to just give it up. Give me a chance. Please!"

Susan hesitated. This intensity of emotion frightened her. What could Maggie say that could change her availability? Yet there was something that kept her from closing the door completely. Susan nodded, agreeing they would talk later, but silently putting up the familiar barriers to her emotions.

Maggie finally smiled and hastily wiped her tears. She rarely cried, and yet Susan could make her so vulnerable it scared her.

Susan took a deep breath. "We must be a mess. I'm sure someone in my family will notice."

"I don't know." Maggie returned Susan's smile. "No one has knocked at the door, no phones or door bells have rung."

They headed back to the kitchen. Susan wanted emotional and physical distance from the roller coaster feelings. These were still too new for her to even try to understand.

Dinner was no relief for Susan. Betsy kept watching and questioning. When Tom recalled reading some article about Maggie and her husband but couldn't remember details, Maggie appeared flustered. Susan noticed the speed with which she quickly and successfully changed the subject. This piqued her curiosity and made her wonder what it was that Maggie wanted to tell her. She tried to come to some logical conclusion—a pending divorce, marital problems. Slowly, she allowed her always fertile imagination to wander down a more wished-for road.

Shortly after dinner, Maggie's cell phone rang and she took the call in the back bedroom. When Maggie returned to the family room, she said, "That was Paul, my husband's...our attorney. He's in Orlando and wants to know if he can drop by for a while. I wasn't sure how to give him directions." Maggie hesitated. "Is it okay if he comes over, and can someone tell him how to get here?"

Tom took her phone and gave directions. "He should be here in less than thirty minutes. He's at the rental car pick-up at the airport."

Susan looked at the clock. At two thirty in the afternoon, she had already had a long, emotional day. She wasn't sure what else she could handle.

Nearly an hour later there was a knock on the door. Maggie offered to answer it. When she opened the door, there was an attractive, smiling man. "Paul, come in. Let me introduce you to my hostess." It was obvious from their hug that they were close and affectionate. Maggie led him to Susan. "Paul, this is my hostess and new friend. Susan Hettinger, this is Paul Williams, my good friend, my attorney, and my one-time savior."

"Susan, it's a pleasure to finally meet you. Maggie sings your praises." Paul took Susan's hand and held it while examining her closely. "She failed to mention how attractive you are, though." He glared at Maggie, but it was still a caring look. "I wonder if there are other things she has also forgotten to tell."

"Thank you. I'm not sure I deserve the compliment, but I'll take it as it was meant. My mother—"

"Hello, I'm Susan's mom. And you are?" Her mother looped her arm into Paul's and gently led him into the living room. "We were just watching the football game. Come on and join us. Looks like a good game."

Susan stared at her mom, amazed that she even knew it was a football game. Susan and her mom had often gone shopping, cooked, or cleaned other rooms while her dad sat in front of the television watching college and professional football. She followed the small group back into the living room. *This day can't get more bizarre.*

Conversation became animated when Paul announced Derek was flying in later in the evening. Tom was ecstatic, Maggie was silent, and Susan admitted the day could get worse, and had. Susan's normally quiet Thanksgiving had turned into an interactive event with too many people to keep track of.

"Derek won't be here until around nine tonight," Paul said. "I'm afraid we'll need to get the kids settled at the hotel before then."

"Nonsense," Susan's mother interrupted. "Let the kids play for a while longer. We have lots of food. Have him come by here and have dinner first."

Paul's efforts to arrange a different outcome were thwarted. Susan knew her mother's love of adventure would ensure

Derek Baxter made an appearance. Her mom knew nothing about football, but Susan was sure that would be the topic of conversation at her mother's ladies' lunch. *The day has been a disaster. Why should tonight be any different?*

Chapter Seven

Maggie was hungry. In spite of only four hours' sleep, she was happy and relieved. Derek had arrived at Susan's shortly after nine p.m. and attempted to get Maggie, the kids, and Paul headed back to the hotel. He was outmaneuvered by Maureen, who was determined to keep the odd ensemble together and had reset the table. After introductions, she herded the adults back into the dining room, while the younger children were put to bed. *Great tactical maneuver. Can't leave without the kids,* Maggie reminded herself. In all the confusion of the evening, Maureen even managed to find her camera and take pictures.

Tom, Kyle, and Derek talked football incessantly and planned a fishing trip for the next summer. Betsy, however, sounding more like a lawyer than a physician, lost no time in asking questions, some subtle, some not. It was obvious Betsy would get information one way or another.

It was midnight before they got settled back in the hotel suite. Paul excused himself and left them to talk.

"I've got to admit," Derek stretched out on one of the chairs in the living area, "this is certainly one of the strangest situations you have ever gotten yourself into." He paused to look at Maggie, sitting silently across from him. "What's going on?"

"God, I've never had to really behave before. I really like her, Derek."

"What do you want from her?"

She thought about Derek's question and wondered what she could offer someone like Susan. Susan was probably a woman who wanted commitment and stability. Maggie remembered the jokes she used to make. *Monogamy—isn't that some type of hardwood?* In the past she'd closely associated sex with drugs, drinking, and instant gratification. At some point in her life, things had changed. She couldn't really remember why or when. Now she wondered if she could be the kind of person Susan wanted.

"Susan is the nicest person you've been involved with in a long time. I'm not trying to sound mean, but are you ready to make that type of commitment? She seems very, well, I guess, traditional."

Maggie hated hearing her own thoughts put into words. She feared the changes she saw happening around her. Derek was slowly moving away from her as his life with Paul grew. "I don't know. A couple of days ago I was remembering Paula. You know, I thought we would be together forever. I really loved her. What went wrong?" Tears threatened.

"If you remember, you were more interested in your career. The travel, the music, and the groupies." He leaned over and put his arms around her and let her cry. "She was staying home studying, being faithful. She was making plans for a future. You were out doing...well, I think your comment was 'too many women and too little time.' She finally decided she didn't like waiting up wondering if you were coming home. She may have stopped trusting you, but it was a long time before she stopped loving you. I love you, Mags. There have been times I haven't approved of what, or whom, you did. I certainly wouldn't have met Paul except for your rather unconventional behavior." Maggie groaned and tried to refrain from smiling. "If you want to explore a relationship with Susan, go ahead. But, and this is a big one, she's not like the other women in your life. Be honest with her. And respect her. I think she genuinely cares about you."

Maggie sat back. She put her near empty bottle down. *Does Susan really care?* "I do care about her."

"I know you do, Mags. See what she's feeling. Don't be afraid to talk to her." Maggie smile and promised. After saying good night, she paced her room for an hour before falling into a dream-filled sleep.

Maggie's thoughts were interrupted by the arrival of breakfast, followed quickly by Maya, her assistant, and finally Paul. Paul briefed her on information he gained from the background check on Susan. He provided detailed information about Susan, her family, and her employer. As usual, he had been thorough in his investigation. Susan sounded like a Girl Scout. Her boss, Ed, however, sounded interesting. A plan began to emerge.

Chapter Eight

Susan, please help me with this." Once again Ed was obsessed with his search for some rock star. "Can't you call a few friends, please!"

"Ed, I am not a drug rehab counselor."

"But you must have friends who are. You know how to get information."

Susan's active imagination jumped in. *I'm caught between a rock singer and a heart place. Very clever, Susan.* "Ed, I always regret getting involved in these things. What is so important about—what's her name again? I got you the list of rehab places."

"M.J. Carson is the lead singer in the band Reckless." Ed stopped and stared at her, "Susan, have you noticed that you've been extremely distracted lately? We discussed her last Monday. She's looking for backing for an independent production company. Come on, just a little help. This could be a really big contact."

Susan glared. She was the financial person, not the glad-hander.

Before she could answer him, a chauffeur in a crisp dark uniform entered the office. It was enough of a distraction for Ed to investigate, leaving all previous discussion unfinished. *And women are accused of being nosy.* Susan's enjoyment of the reprieve from questioning was short-lived. A few minutes later

Ed was walking back toward her with a strange look on his face. This did not look good. *Do they now send limousines to tell you someone has died?* Susan wondered. "It's for you. There's a gentleman and a lady waiting in the limo to take you to lunch. I mean us. Who is it, Susan?"

To lunch? Do they feed you and then tell you the bad news?

She couldn't remember standing up, but she was walking out of her office. The chauffeur was holding the front door open. Susan remembered that at her father's funeral, there was always someone opening and closing doors. With each step she tried to remember what bad news could be waiting for her. Her mother had looked well that morning. She didn't think they would send a car from Jacksonville if something happened to Tom or Betsy. She stopped at the door, confused. When she looked around she found Ed, the receptionist, and most of the staff following. She felt like the mother duckling in *Make Way for Ducklings*, her daughter's favorite book. Only this time it was more like make way for way-too-curious ducklings.

The stretch limo parked at the curb did not provide any clues as to the identity of the people inside. At that point, Susan didn't want to know. When the chauffeur opened the limo door, Paul stepped out. Susan didn't need to see the face of the other person. She recognized the legs. Seeing them meant that her work, her place of sanctuary, had joined her world of chaos.

Maggie leaned forward and flashed her incredible smile. Susan's throat tightened as one long leg exited the door, followed by the second. Susan felt a gentle pulsing beginning in a very private area of her body. She remained immobile, not sure she could trust her body. Finally Maggie was standing in front of Ed. Maggie extended her hand.

"Hello. I hope I'm not interrupting your day."

"Hi, I'm Ed...Ms. Carson? M.J. Carson?" The astonished look on Ed's face quickly changed to one of delight.

Susan stared. *M.J. Carson? Maggie Carson-Baxter. Is*

Maggie the person Ed has been looking for? Ed's comments floated randomly, drugs, sex rumors, legal troubles. *No, this can't be my Maggie! Wait, when did she become "my" Maggie?*

"Yes. And you must be Ed Howard. I have heard quite a bit about you. Susan sings your praises." Maggie put her sunglasses back on, but she couldn't hide that warm grin.

Everyone stared at Susan. She wanted to wiggle her nose and disappear, but there was no magic today. Maggie continued with introductions."This is my attorney, Paul Williams. I was hoping the four of us could have lunch and maybe talk some business. Susan insists you're the person we need."

The grin that spread across Ed's face underlined his excitement. As he led the group back toward his office, Ed introduced Maggie to the staff. Several asked for autographs. That was just enough diversion for Ed to pull Susan aside and demand to know why she denied knowing M.J. Carson. She pleaded ignorance. Strangely, Ed believed her. The other members of the staff stared. Susan wondered if her zipper was open or if her hair had changed color. It didn't matter, she wanted to hide. Instead she quietly followed the procession to Ed's corner office while the receptionist made reservations for lunch.

The trip to the restaurant and the lunch were a blur. At first Susan sat numb and listened to Paul and Ed discuss business with frequent commentary by Maggie. As she listened, however, she was impressed with Maggie's knowledge and detail in her business ventures. Any other time, she would be thrilled to be sitting in a small alcove overlooking Lake Eola, next to an attractive woman, discussing business. Today her emotions were flying all over the place.

As they finished lunch, Maggie ordered a bottle of Perrier Jouët. As the champagne was poured, she said, "To a profitable venture for all of us." After sipping from her glass, she turned to Ed. "I'm impressed with what you have done and what you may be able to do for us. I want to make sure, however, you thoroughly understand what I plan, how I operate, and what I want to do. I would like Susan to work closely, at least for the next month, with me, or my assistant, and learn my operation."

Susan fought to contain her response. "We have other staff we generally assign to handle this sort of detail. I don't handle production."

Maggie had her own agenda. "But you have such a keen mind and would be able to provide guidance in our planning." Paul and Ed sat quietly. "I want this to be successful, and you're the one that can do it. Besides," Maggie covered Susan's hand, "I trust you."

Susan stared at Maggie...no, M.J. Carson. Did she really know who this person was? No matter her personal feelings, Susan realized this was business. Knowing this was a losing battle, she gritted her teeth. "Of course."

"Well, if that's decided, Ed and I will go draw up preliminary contracts while you two discuss details." Paul stood, promising to send the limo back.

"Susan, I'm excited. We have so much to talk about," Maggie said.

Oh, really! Susan doubted there was much to talk about. *And I have some swamp land in Colorado I want to sell.* "Look, Maggie, I don't know what's going on. If you feel you owe me something, you don't. I really need to get back to work as soon as the limo gets back."

"Susan, can you just listen?"

For what? So you can have a few more laughs at my expense? Susan managed to keep the conversation impersonal until they were in the car. "Look, Maggie...M.J., whatever your name is. I appreciate you giving your business to my boss, but you don't owe me anything. We can find someone else to travel with you. I really don't know anything about production, and I would prefer not traveling."

Maggie rolled up the window behind the driver and took her

hand. "This must all be confusing. I promise you there is more to be explained. Just trust me a little longer."

Susan blinked at the use of the word trust. She pulled her hand away. *Trust! That's a mouthful for someone...* Susan stopped. *For someone who...* "You don't owe me any explanations. I do need to get back to work as soon as possible."

When they arrived at the office, Maggie held on to her hand. "Just stay in the car, please."

After picking up Paul, Maggie again tried to hold Susan's hand. Paul didn't mind, or didn't notice. Susan noticed and quickly slipped her hand back into her own lap. She leaned away making her hands, and body, out of reach.

At the hotel, they were escorted to a special elevator and to a suite high above Disney. A uniformed guard opened the door to a cacophony of children, phones, and voices raised in discussion. Shortly after their arrival, everyone except Derek, Paul, Maggie, and Susan was herded out of the room. Susan's imagination took off. Looking at Derek, she wondered, *Does he know what happened? Is he going to be the aggrieved husband? Is he threatening a divorce?* Life had become like riding Space Mountain; she never knew where the next hill would end or begin.

Maggie sat next to Susan on the couch, which sent Susan's blood pressure soaring. Paul leaned on the arm of Derek's chair. Susan's stomach rumbled. *Maybe I can throw up and that will change the topic.*

Maggie spoke first. "Susan, Paul is my attorney and a really close friend, but he is also Derek's lover."

"I know he's your—" Susan stopped and looked across at the two men. Only then did she notice the casual way Paul's arm draped across Derek's shoulder, the way they looked at each other. Turning back to Maggie, she asked, "He's what? Is this some kind of California thing?"

"No, it's an NFL thing," Derek answered, laughing. "Our

sophomore year I met Maggie in a gay bar. We started hanging out together. Maggie was comfortable with her sexuality and I was scared shitless. Growing up, I internalized enough of my parents' homophobic ideas, they became my own." Derek turned toward Maggie and the look spoke volumes about the depth of their relationship. "Maggie did more than provide a cover for me, she helped me deal with my own sexuality. She's my best friend."

Maggie's eyes glistened.

"So, my senior year, when I knew I was going to go high in the NFL draft, we decided to get married. Fifteen years ago, I would have been a pariah, and now I've been able to have a great career. She's been successful in her music career. It's worked well for both of us."

He reached for Paul's hand. "Then four years ago, I met Paul and life became a little more complicated. Paul knew up front we were both gay. I apologize if you feel deceived. You see, there are many people who've taken advantage of Maggie's celebrity status or her generosity."

The full import of this message floated in the cobwebs of Susan's mind. Holding Maggie's hand, kissing her—all this time feeling guilty. Suddenly many of their conversations had new meaning, a different interpretation. *The whole time I was sitting and apologizing to Maggie, she must have been having a great laugh.*

The quiet was broken by Derek, excusing himself, saying he was sure we had much to talk about. He and Paul left.

Maggie tried to move closer, but Susan stood and walked away. "Please say something," Maggie said.

Susan was numb. Once again, she recalled Ed's comments: rumors of divorce, M.J.'s playing around, drugs. Was she just a fling? Some brief entertainment? She had difficulty fitting all this information into the orderly world in which she lived. Had Maggie lied? Was Maggie just playing a game? Could Susan trust her?

"Susan, please talk to me."

Susan finally turned and looked at Maggie. *Who is this woman? What does she really want?* With no ready answers, Susan opted for the more familiar. "Maggie, could you please have someone drive me back to my office? I have a lot of work to finish this afternoon."

CHAPTER NINE

Of all the possible reactions, this was not one Maggie had anticipated. Had she mistaken Susan's interest? "Susan, don't you understand? There's no reason we can't be with each other."

"Yes, there is. Now will you please take me back to work?"

No one had ever told Maggie no. "Just sit. If you don't want to pursue a personal relationship, then I must remind you that we have a business one. I'll have my assistant come in and we'll start," she said, turning to the phone.

Susan struggled with her tumultuous feelings. She remained silent except when asked a question. Her answers were short and to the point. Only when informed that she would be accompanying Maggie to Atlanta for a concert the next day did she protest. "Maggie, I can't just abandon my family on short notice. If you want me to review financial records, I'll be glad to do that from my office."

"I expect you to be available whenever I need you," Maggie said. "I'll call Maureen, Ed, and anyone else. Now, let's finish our business." Forty minutes later Maya left to finalize their travel arrangements.

Susan couldn't remember ever being this angry. Accustomed to controlling her actions and emotions, she just wanted to run out of the damn room, but she wanted it to be a graceful run. At this point she wasn't sure she was capable of that much coordination. "If we're finished, I need to go home, pack, and spend some time with my family."

❖

Maggie wanted Susan, but she knew Susan had to come freely. To get beyond the business side of Susan, Maggie had to be patient, a characteristic she had never mastered.

The next day the private jet was loaded and waiting when Maggie and Susan boarded. Maggie provided introductions. "This is Karl. He's been my manager for four years. Outlasted all the previous ones. Guess I pay him well." Karl rolled his eyes while shaking Susan's hand. "This is Jeremy. He and I formed Reckless eight years ago. He's the drummer, and a damn good one."

"And I put up with all her bad jokes. Glad to meet you."

Susan remembered briefly meeting Maya, Maggie's assistant, and said hello. Susan doubted she would remember most of the rest of the crew.

In Atlanta, the entire top two floors of the Peachtree World Resort had been reserved for Maggie's entourage. In spite of Susan's protests, Maggie insisted they share a large two-bedroom corner suite.

"I'm sure you want to meet with your own staff later, and I'll want to sleep. I'll arrange for my own room." Susan started to walk up to the desk.

"Susan, we'll be sharing a large two-bedroom suite and you will have your privacy. I..." Maggie hesitated, choosing her words carefully. "I would appreciate having you nearby... to consult with or answer any questions about our business." Sighing, she realized Susan wasn't smiling and the twinkle in her eye was dimmed. "I also want to get to know you better. I don't have a lot of experience with this friendship thing, but I really want to try."

Susan stared at Maggie, fidgeting with the ring on her finger, then shoving her hands in her pocket, and finally nervously running her fingers through her hair. *Could Maggie be as uncomfortable as I am?* She nodded. "I guess I can put up with a suite for a couple of nights."

A corner of Maggie's mouth lifted in a hopeful smile.

❖

Shortly after settling into their hotel rooms, they headed for the theater and a dress rehearsal. Maggie thrived in the intense, hectic pace of the evening. The music, the tension, and even the atmosphere ignited the passion within her. She absorbed the energy and it came back out in a raw sexuality. Susan was mesmerized.

When Susan was introduced as a financial consultant, people gave her a blank smile and said, "How nice." Like "The archipelago represented interesting biodiversity." How nice. Susan quickly learned what the word "groupie" meant. How nice.

A tall, thin man named Dan introduced himself, welcoming them to Atlanta. "Ms. Carson, thank you for sponsoring this fund-raiser. I can't tell you how much AIDS Atlanta appreciates you stepping in and pulling this together. When Elton John had to cancel, we didn't know what we would do. Then Karl called and said you would do the show and sponsor the entire thing."

Susan stared at a blushing Maggie. *Sponsoring? An AIDS fund-raiser?* She felt more confused. There was much more to Maggie than Susan imagined. As Dan introduced the board members, Maggie greeted each person, quietly walking around shaking hands, not hesitating in hugging or touching.

While Maggie spent time talking individually to the board, Dan walked up to Susan. "She's amazing."

"Yes," Susan said.

"She's done so much for our community. And most of the

time, she does things quietly. There are probably only two or three people who know she's footing the entire bill. It's become fashionable in some large cities to sponsor AIDS fund-raisers. M.J. does more. She really cares. She's also a big sponsor of breast cancer awareness. I think her mother died of breast cancer when M.J. was young. With her these issues are personal, not just another headlining opportunity."

Karl then appeared, urging M.J. and the band to get on stage. Many of the other performers and visitors settled into seats, choosing to remain for the entire rehearsal. Susan was on overload. Who was this woman?

Maggie walked up to Susan. "Will you sit on the stage and wait for me?"

Susan nodded. "Thanks. I'd like that."

Throughout the rehearsal Maggie glanced over at Susan, actually walking off stage twice to smile or wink. Susan's heart and head were at war. Unable to handle the conflicting emotions, she slipped into the audience, hoping to sort through her feelings. When Maggie next walked to the left side of the stage, she stumbled over her music as she searched for Susan. Every few minutes she searched the backstage area, but she did not stop the rehearsal. This caused comments from people in the audience, wondering what, or who, she was looking for. Finally, at eleven, the band quit.

Susan wanted to be alone, but those left at the end of rehearsal were hungry and thirsty. Dan recommended a local deli and the band, other entertainers, Maggie, and her staff descended on the place. Conversation was loud and animated. Maggie glowed in the attention and admiration but she was also considerate, even gentle with fans who sought her attention.

As she walked around, Maggie spent time at every table. "I am so glad you could join us this evening. What do you folks do in Atlanta?" Maggie sat and listened to them describe their jobs.

The next group she joined was a local all-women rock band.

"I want you to know how much I enjoy your music," she said. "I didn't recognize it. Are you performing your own stuff?"

The woman with spiked red hair answered, "Yeah, we are. Thank you. That means a lot. I write most of it, but some of it we write as a group." Maggie made each person feel important, as if no one else mattered.

"Hold on. Maya!" She called her assistant over and introduced her to the group. "Maya, will you give them one of your cards and be sure to get their names and phone numbers. We're going into the production business and we would like for you to consider recording on our label."

Susan admired Maggie's ability to be such an engaging hostess. She no longer knew what to believe about Maggie. Her well of reserve was being drained quickly.

As if reading Susan's mind, Maggie slid into the booth and whispered, "I'm ready to leave. How about you?" Susan nodded, realizing she had become a nonverbal idiot. Around Maggie, she had trouble remembering her own name. Maggie took her hand and helped her out of the booth. Thirty minutes later, they were alone in the room.

Susan tried to escape to her bedroom but was short-circuited by a quicker Maggie as she stepped in front of the door. A seductive smile spread across Maggie's face. Susan stepped back. Maggie moved closer. They continued this two-step until Susan backed into a wall. Maggie leaned one arm against the wall and moved against Susan.

"When you disappeared off the stage," Maggie said, "I had a moment of panic. I missed you. Tomorrow will you promise to stay backstage?"

Susan took a deep breath and agreed. She was confused. *Why is it that every time this woman comes near me, all my bodily systems go into overdrive and my brain goes on vacation?*

Maggie leaned closer. Susan was well aware of what would happen next. The touch of Maggie's lips was as soft and gentle as

Susan remembered. Maggie barely brushed her lips over Susan's. She pulled away, but only inches, searching for any hesitancy. Susan met her eyes and did not turn away. Finding an answer, Maggie's next kiss was not nearly as tentative. It was urgent, demanding.

Susan's body responded to the probing tongue. A low moan escaped as Susan opened and welcomed her in. An incredible hunger started in her center and spread until Susan wondered how she remained standing. She pulled Maggie closer and felt the soft swell of her breasts. Susan was drowning in such exquisite hunger.

Maggie caressed the back of Susan's neck as she trailed kisses down her chin and neck before moving back up to recapture her lips. Susan drank in the tenderness. Never had she wanted anyone as much as she wanted Maggie. As she started to unbutton Maggie's shirt, Maggie pulled back.

"Not tonight. I don't want you to have any regrets. Not just because you may be tired. Not in one moment of passion." She stroked Susan's cheek. "Good night. I'll see you in a few hours." She placed one more gentle kiss, turned, and walked into the other bedroom, closing the door behind her. Susan stood there breathless.

Getting to sleep wasn't easy. Maggie scared her.

Maggie closed the door behind her and leaned against it, afraid to turn around. She couldn't believe she had walked away from Susan. What was happening? She wasn't sure she would know how to handle involvement without her old crutches. What would she do if Susan still said yes tomorrow? Sleep eluded her. Too many questions swirled in her dreams. For the first time in a long time, Maggie was confused and afraid.

CHAPTER TEN

Maggie was up long before her eight a.m. wake-up call, her adrenaline rush preventing sleep. She had arranged for an early call at the theater so the band could get in, set up, and do their checks before the other acts were even on their way to the theater. By noon they would be out of there and could rest until their evening performance.

During the tech rehearsal, Maggie oversaw every lighting and special effects cue. She planned each light fade, color change, and special effect. This complete control gave her a high that drugs used to provide. *Better than sex*, she once told Derek. Already she was feeling aroused. For the first part of the rehearsal, she sat behind the technician at the master console and watched the cues scroll by on the computer screen as her band moved quickly through the set. "Right here I want the drummer's mike on," she said, pointing to the screen. "This dialogue is between the drummer and me. Fade the lights except our two spots. Make it a gradual fade." The tech nodded, asked the band to hold, and made the changes. The band restarted. "No, that's too fast. I don't want the audience to really notice the fade out." Again, the band started over. "That's it. Now, here." She pointed to the next lighting cue, offering another change. After going through the entire show and reviewing all the spots, she rejoined her band onstage. At twelve fifteen, she and her staff were on their way back to the hotel.

While Maggie often preferred to be alone before concerts, today she was restless and unsure of the welcome she would have when she returned to her suite. "Maya, come up so we can finalize the plans for the CD." Maggie ignored the surprised look on Maya's face and continued talking as they went up in the elevator.

When they arrived in the room, Maggie found it empty. Even though Susan left a note saying she would be back at five, Maggie had trouble focusing. Finally, at two, she sent Maya off to her own room. *Where the hell is she?* Maggie wasn't accustomed to worrying about someone she barely knew. By the time Susan returned at four thirty, Maggie was irrational.

"Where the hell have you been?" Maggie shouted. "You can't wander around Atlanta and not let anyone know where you are or when the fuck you will be back."

Refusing to look at Maggie, Susan answered calmly, "Hello. Glad to see you. Yes, I had a great day." She slowly sorted through objects in the bags she carried.

"Jesus H. Christ." Maggie grabbed Susan, forcing her to turn and face her. Susan pulled her arm away and crossed her arms. "I've been worried sick wondering if you were okay, where you were, if you were coming back."

"Well, as you can see, I'm fine."

"Damn it, Susan. I have a concert tonight. I don't need this." Maggie sighed, her anger spent. Somewhere underneath the rage, Maggie recognized her fear was unreasonable, but she was unable, or unwilling, to acknowledge those feelings.

"First," Susan began in a barely controlled tone, "I left a note telling you I was going out and when I would be back. Second, I didn't ask to come to Atlanta. I was ordered. Third, as if it's any of your business, I visited a friend from college and invited her to the concert and the dance, unless you have a problem with that. Finally, I am not responsible for your anger. Excuse me, I need to shower and change."

Maggie immediately regretted her behavior. "I'm sorry. You

don't owe me any explanations." Susan nodded and started to walk away. "Please, wait." Susan halted. "I said I'm sorry."

Susan nodded. "Apology accepted." She walked into her room and closed the door.

❖

Leaning against her door, Susan muttered, "What an ego. 'I don't need this.' Well, neither do I." She put her packages down. "I don't care how important her account may be to Ed, I am not going anywhere else with this egomaniac." Susan briefly wondered how she had gotten into this. "That woman is infuriating." Her words didn't negate the attraction. "Damn you, Maggie!"

Showered and dressed, Susan gathered the remnants of her fragile control. "I wonder if this emotional roller coaster is what menopause is like. If it is, then shoot me now and put me out of my misery."

When she walked into the sitting room, Maggie was dressed in form-fitting black leather pants, shiny black knee-high boots, and a revealing black leather vest. Susan stared at the soft swell of breasts. She balled her hands into fists to keep from reaching out and touching. Susan took a deep breath, not sure her legs would continue to support her. She forced herself to look away, and that's when she noticed the flowers. Flowers filled every inch of the room with a rainbow of color.

"They're beautiful."

"It took a little work," Maggie said. "I didn't know what kind or color you liked, so I tried to get a dozen of everything." Maggie was now inches away. She lifted Susan's palm and kissed it. "I know there's no real excuse for my behavior earlier. I screwed up. I'm sorry. I was so afraid something might have happened to you. Give me another chance, please. You're probably tired of my asking for another chance, but I am trying."

Maggie's eyes filled with tears, but she never looked away.

That unexpected vulnerability surprised Susan, and she wanted to fix the hurt. The roller coaster was headed up again, and Susan knew she was losing control. "Maggie, these flowers are nice, but…" She struggled for the right words. There was pain in Maggie's eyes. Susan lightly rested her hand on top of Maggie's. "I may regret this, but you get one more chance." Maggie wrapped Susan in an embrace.

They were soon back at the theater and the level of excitement had escalated. Dan and several men in tuxedos escorted them to Maggie's dressing room. As soon as the door closed behind them, Maggie whispered, "This really means a lot to me."

Susan felt the words more than heard them. Maggie's voice was soft and sensual. Her body felt caressed without being touched.

"If I get a chair for you, will you sit near the stage where I can see you?"

Susan nodded. Maggie moved closer and she had trouble breathing. Maggie captured her lips. The kiss was urgent.

Maggie pushed against Susan's body. She caressed Susan's face before sliding down to her shoulders. Maggie kissed down the neck until clothes prevented further exploration. A groan slipped from Susan before she could stop it.

"Thank you for being here tonight. I'm so sorry about earlier."

"Maggie, I—" Maggie's hand covered Susan's lips.

"Don't say anything. Not yet." Maggie's words were barely a whisper and Susan felt her heart start to open.

A knock at the door broke the spell. The hair stylist entered, chattering about various Atlanta nightspots. For the next fifteen minutes he arranged her hair and her makeup before attaching a headset. Maggie was transformed into a different creature than the one Susan knew. She was now M.J. Carson.

Five minutes before their set, Maggie had someone bring Susan to the backstage area where a stool had been placed for her. She could see the stage, but not the audience. As the band entered and the music began, Susan felt strong arms encircle her from behind. She recognized Maggie's scent.

"Again, thank you," Maggie said, then she was bouncing out on the stage, reaching for her guitar as the crowd screamed her name.

During the next forty minutes, Maggie was boundless energy, constantly moving, dancing. Susan was amazed by her sheer sexuality. At times, Maggie walked to the side of the stage, just a few feet away, and sang. Her music was sultry and husky and then frantic and uncontrolled. She closed her eyes and leaned her head back, her body taut with sexual promise. She was making love to the audience with her music, and they responded.

Susan was embarrassed by the rawness, yet she couldn't prevent her own response. The fire Susan suspected was inside Maggie had become a consuming inferno with no escape for those in her path. The temperature in the auditorium was at the combustible level.

Near the end of their first set, Maggie came off the stage and ran with Susan to her dressing room. The door closed behind them. They listened to the band finish the set as Maggie pulled her clothes off. Five minutes later she had changed and was ready for the next set. When she heard the overhead stage call she realized they had a few minutes. "Five minutes," she said as she pulled Susan into an embrace. Her kiss was again possessive. The heat of that one kiss shook Susan as no other ever had. Everywhere Susan's body touched Maggie's felt singed. Briefly Susan imagined she could smell the smoke.

"I want you," said Maggie. Susan was sure the smoke detectors were going off. Maggie grinned and grabbed her headset. "Show time," she said. "Let's go."

Susan wanted to ask where but she didn't care anymore.

The second set started with a slow, sensuous blues number. When the song finished, Maggie talked to the crowd. "The band just finished recording a new CD. When I was growing up, I loved to listen to love songs, and I always wanted to sing them to a special someone." She looked at Susan sitting off stage, then turned her attention to the shouting audience. "Our new CD, *Special Someone*, will be out next February. We're going to do a couple of songs from that CD."

The drummer's pulsing beat echoed through the auditorium, an amplified heartbeat. The keyboard's melody began softly at first, followed by the lead guitar. The backup vocalists humming blended with the instruments. Maggie lifted the microphone to her lips. The song was filled with wanting. Susan felt the music in her soul.

At the end of their second set, they were called back and played for another ten minutes before finally leaving the stage. The house lights on, everyone headed back to Maggie's dressing room, which was now filled with people, alcohol, and snack food. Susan quietly moved into a corner and watched. Maggie was everywhere, talking, laughing, her hands constantly in motion. Susan would have felt completely out of place if she wasn't so turned on by thinking how those hands would feel on her body.

After twenty minutes of raucous chaos, Karl reminded the crowd they needed to get to the dance and Maggie needed to change. He managed to empty the room in spite of one or two stragglers who were determined to be alone with M.J. Carson.

Maggie quickly showered and changed into a green silk blouse, jeans, and a navy blue blazer. She was somewhere between M.J. and Maggie and still stunning. The front of the blouse was open to just above her waist, a very provocative, and intentional, effect.

Susan had always considered herself asexual at worst and a depressed libido at best. Maggie reminded her that she was not dead. Maggie grabbed her hand and said, "Let's dance." Susan thought they already were.

Chapter Eleven

The ballroom at the hotel was packed. This didn't prevent Maggie from being noticed. She shook hands, signed autographs, and chatted as she gradually made her way to a reserved table. She was the glad-handing politician. For the next hour, she danced with Dan, Karl, Maya, and even a few strangers, unable to gather the courage to ask Susan, the only person she really wanted to dance with.

Susan began to question her decision to participate in this madness. Maggie had practically ignored her since their arrival at the dance. Only when her friend Nancy arrived was she able to relax. Nancy wasted no time getting Susan on the dance floor.

"Do you have any idea how difficult it has been to get tickets? This has been sold out for over a month. When you showed up today and offered a pass, I thought you were kidding. How did you get to be part of this group?" Nancy was one of the few lesbian friends Susan had maintained since college. And Nancy had been one of the most supportive.

"My company is representing Ms. Carson."

"Are the rumors true?" Nancy leaned closer and whispered, "Is she? You know. What is she like?"

Susan was cautious in her answer. "She is talented and intelligent." Nancy expectantly waited for more. "It's strictly professional." Nancy opened her mouth as if to speak but closed it quickly. "Really, Nancy, this is a professional relationship." Susan cursed herself for the half-truth. Nancy changed the topic to catch up on friends and life.

Four dances later, Maggie cut in and wasted no time in asking questions. "Who is that? She's good looking. I assume she's a lesbian."

"She's a good friend from college. Remember I mentioned I visited her today? We roomed together for two years and have been friends since."

"Were you more than roommates?" Maggie asked.

Could jealousy be tickling? "Yes."

Maggie glared at Nancy. "Is there something still going on between you two now?"

"Yes." Susan spoke slowly, enjoying the emotions dancing across Maggie's face. "We're friends. Just friends."

Maggie stopped dancing. "Nothing sexual, nothing romantic?"

Susan shook her head.

"Just friends?" Again Susan agreed. A smile broke across Maggie's face as she pulled Susan close and resumed dancing. "I'm going to have to watch you. You have a wicked sense of humor." After one more dance, they returned to the reserved table.

A female admirer quickly jumped at the chance to ask Maggie to dance. Much to the woman's obvious delight, Maggie said yes.

Nancy slipped into the seat next to Susan. "Don't hand me that client routine, Susan. My question should have been, what's going on between you two?"

"Funny, Maggie was asking me the same question about you. Maybe you two should talk to each other. I'll tell you the same thing I told her. We're just friends."

"Hot friend, Susan. I never pictured you as a media groupie."

"I am not a groupie," Susan said. "Damn it, Nancy, we're

just friends. There's nothing going on between us." *Yet.* Susan surprised herself with this thought.

Before Nancy could ask another question, Maggie again pulled Susan onto the dance floor.

Susan abandoned any attempt at coherent conversation. She drowned in the sensuality of their dancing. It was beyond suggestive. For once Susan allowed her senses to revel in the intensity of the moment. Maggie whispered in Susan's ear. Her hips ground against Susan. Every inch of Susan's body responded. She tried to convince herself this didn't mean anything, but certain parts of her body weren't cooperating. Maggie inserted her knee between Susan's legs and slid up and down, her eyes never wavering. This was a new dance for Susan, but she suspected where it led. For the next two songs, everything else faded. There was only Maggie, only this closeness, only this fire growing within her, only this consuming need.

At the end of the song, Maggie pulled back and grabbed Susan's hand, walking up to the front where the band played. Maggie joined the band on stage. The crowd quieted.

"I want to thank you for making this an exciting and profitable evening for AIDS Atlanta. I understand we set a new record tonight, for attendance and money raised." Applause filled the hall. "We must never forget why we are here. There are still diseases that tear apart our lives. Until these diseases no longer exist we must continue to fight them and conquer them. We're getting closer but we're not there yet." Maggie smiled at the cheering crowd. "The band and I just finished a new CD that has a special love song. So hold on to that someone special."

The band began to play. Maggie began to sing. Susan knew it was ridiculous, but she felt as if Maggie was singing to her. *Everyone here probably feels that way.* As she looked around, she watched couples dancing and smiling. *Yes, they can feel that same heat.*

There was a moment of quiet while the audience absorbed the final pulsing chords. Lovers catching their breath. The reaction was deafening, but Maggie could only see Susan standing near the stage. She acknowledged the applause and waved. After giving a thumbs-up to the band, Maggie grabbed Susan's hand and they were headed out of the ballroom. Susan had forgotten everything but Maggie—her scent, her touch, her fire.

With Karl and Dan leading the charge, they were soon in the elevator and headed upstairs. At last they were alone. Maggie closed the door. As the lock clicked shut Susan realized there would be no interruptions, no door bells, no phone calls. She was both nervous and excited. She feared she would be found wanting as a lover but also knew she wanted Maggie more than she had wanted anyone. She silently prayed that Maggie wouldn't be disappointed.

Maggie offered Susan a glass of wine. Her fingers barely grazed Susan's. She walked around the bar and stood behind Susan, leaning forward, putting her head against Susan's. "I can't tell you how many times I wanted to just put my arms around you," she said. "As I sang tonight, I sang for you, about you, with you. I want to make love with you. I think I have since the first night at your house." She caressed Susan's back, pulling her closer. "Are you aware of how beautiful you are? Or how desirable?" Susan shook her head. "No matter what I want, Susan, I don't want to do, or say, anything that may cause…" Maggie faltered. "I don't want to lose you." She paused.

"I can't believe I'm saying this but I want you to know it's true. I would rather have you as my friend, and in my life, than to spend one night making love and lose you forever." She had never asked before, much less told someone to say no. Susan was different. She wanted Susan to want her. She wanted her to want Maggie, not M.J.

Susan grabbed a handful of hair and twirled it, enjoying the soft, thick tresses. Breathing was not possible. Thinking required effort. Maggie's mouth was warm and inviting. She had to taste it. This time it was Maggie who was groaning.

Susan led Maggie into the bedroom. M.J. the singer couldn't

remember the last time she had been this nervous, and Maggie the person was petrified. These feelings were too intense.

Susan reached over and began to pull open Maggie's shirt. All night she had wanted to reach in and touch the soft flesh within. Her own daring amazed her.

Maggie allowed Susan to undress her. She leaned her head back and closed her eyes. She held her breath as soft hands touched her body.

Susan's gaze feasted, following the trail of her hands as they touched and caressed Maggie's arms, hips, and then erect nipples. Seeing the growing desire in Maggie's eyes, Susan removed her own blouse and pants.

Maggie's knees began to tremble. Maggie wanted to see and feel Susan's body, but she feared her ability to control her own pulsing center. Maggie pushed Susan onto the bed and climbed on top. This was heaven, she thought, feeling the softness of Susan beneath her. This first time she wanted to savor. Her own needs, however, were so urgent, she could feel her orgasm approaching.

She placed featherlike kisses on Susan's eyes, then her neck, and her nose, always returning to the lips that attracted her like warm honey. She nibbled down Susan's neck until she found the one place that elicited a moan from Susan. She focused on this area and felt Susan shudder beneath her. Maggie removed the remaining clothing and relished the naked body beneath her. She continued her explorations. Moving on to the soft, rounded breasts, Maggie first covered one with her mouth while she caressed the other. She sucked on a nipple until it became erect inside her mouth. She paused to look into Susan's eyes. She could read the desire and passion as clearly as she could feel it. Maggie felt her own wetness flowing just by looking at Susan. Returning to the swollen breasts, she again tasted one and then moved on to the other, listening to the changes in Susan's breathing. Susan's hands were pulling her back into demanding kisses. Susan stroked her back and flowed down to her buttocks, caressing the flesh, then running fingernails across her back. Maggie mounted Susan's leg, her throbbing too painful to ignore. At first, she moved slowly back and forth, her own wetness coating Susan's thigh. Hands encircling her breasts and squeezing the nipples brought her closer to climax. She realized she was coming too quickly, but she was beyond control. Susan pulled her down and took a breast in her mouth and stroked the nipple with her tongue.

Maggie's movements became more frantic. She craved release. Her body shook as convulsions swept deep inside her. She was stunned by the intensity. Somehow, Susan managed to change positions with Maggie. She reached between Maggie's legs and softly touched her swollen flesh, continually caressing until Maggie was again close to orgasm. Slowly she slid her fingers into the warm wetness. Maggie gasped and began to move with the new rhythm Susan had set. Again and again, the hand moved against her, sliding in and out until Maggie cried out and grasped Susan tightly. After the last wave passed, she could again breathe.

"My God," Maggie gasped, "what happened?" She smiled and then noticed the tears in Susan's eyes. "What's the matter? Did I do something wrong?"

Susan tried to smile but was overwhelmed by her own emotions. "No, you're perfect. You are incredibly beautiful and passionate. It's just so intense."

"I like intense." Maggie leaned up and began to again kiss Susan. "Intense is good." This time she knew she would be able to take her time. "Intense is very good." She switched places with Susan. Susan became a musical instrument Maggie played with passion and precision. She quickly learned the important chords and played them, embellishing and rearranging. Susan's body was a fine instrument, and an erotic song filled the night air. With a gentle hunger, she played different melodies, her own body providing counterpoints. Susan's body began a crescendo of indeterminable length and intensity, led by Maggie as she touched and savored. Those wonderful hands that conducted a conversation were an even more impressive maestro as they orchestrated the passion growing within Susan. Maggie covered Susan with kisses, moving down to her hips, where a most intimate melody was about to achieve completion. Maggie tasted the wetness. Her hand became a bow and Susan was her violin. She played with a fever and intensity that surprised even her.

At last, waves of different color and timbre covered Susan. She let out a cry, like the cymbal crashing, exclaiming the overture's final movement.

Maggie moved up Susan, kissing along the body now glistening with excitement. She reached the warm, tender lips and again drowned herself. Susan was smiling.

"You are incredible," Susan began, then hesitated, looking for the right words. "I know this probably sounds trite, but I didn't know it could be like this."

Maggie smiled. No words could express the power of her feelings or the depth. To put voice to those emotions was terrifying. It was easier to live in the moment, to stay with the song she was playing. She recalled some of the phrases she had recently played. She couldn't get enough. She would play this symphony again and create new variations upon the theme. Susan was easily aroused, this time knowing where the music was leading. They played and replayed their favorite melodies, over and over, reclaiming passion as their muse.

Light filled the room before they were aware of anything but emotions and touching. Susan sat up and looked at the clock. "Maggie, it's nearly seven. We need to get some sleep." Maggie's protests were quick, but so was sleep.

❖

It was many moments before Susan acknowledged the distant drumming as her own heart. She stared at the dark lashes fluttering against the tanned face. *I cannot believe this sleeping, peaceful woman is capable of arousing such passion in me.* Innocence and vulnerability had displaced the cocky, self-assured singer. Maggie was once again the woman she had met on the plane.

Susan's emotions vacillated between fear and love. Fear because she was so out of control. And recognition of the love she had been barely acknowledging all day. *Whom am I kidding? Maggie has occupied my thoughts and dreams since we met. Here I am in bed with someone I've only known three weeks. I've had only two lovers and never even considered sex until we had known each other for months. Yet here I am with you, Maggie. Where are we going? Am I just a temporary diversion? Will you wake up and pretend this was just a meaningless affair? I couldn't stand that.*

CHAPTER TWELVE

The flight back to Orlando was quiet. While Maggie was attentive and affectionate at the hotel, once aboard the plane she quickly fell asleep. Susan's insecurities kicked in as she tried to apply logic to the emotional chaos of the previous day.

Thirty minutes into their flight, Maggie awoke and smiled. "Sorry. Guess something wore me out." One side of her mouth lifted into a most intimate smile. "Or someone." Almost immediately Susan felt heat creep up her neck. "You're so cute when you blush." Maggie gently stroked Susan's cheek.

"Looks like most everyone else is sleeping. Guess it was the concert." Susan hoped Maggie hadn't noticed her awkwardness. Quickly changing the subject, she asked, "How long has your band been together?"

"Is that what you really want to talk about?"

"No."

"Good. Honey, please, no work." Feeling chastised, Susan quietly nodded. Maggie pulled her closer and was soon asleep again, leaving Susan more confused.

The arrival in Orlando at a private airport was organized chaos. Limos parked near the hangar swiftly moved out to the plane. Suitcases of various shapes and sizes lined the tarmac and were haphazardly thrown into the waiting vehicles. After a quick hug, Maggie jumped into a waiting limo with a promise to call later. The driver of the remaining vehicle grabbed Susan's bag and helped her into the car.

Susan felt as if she had been caught up in a tornado and unexpectedly dumped in some cornfield in Kansas without Toto. Her emotions were raw. She was exhausted and confused, and she wanted to sleep. At the same time she dreaded the modern version of the Spanish Inquisition she'd face when she arrived home. Maureen surprised her by not asking many questions. Instead her mother sent her off to bed, with promises to wake her in a couple of hours. At last Susan felt a return of normalcy. As she drifted off to sleep, she reminded herself of how relieved she was to be home.

Susan returned to work in a foul mood. Two days had gone by without any word from Maggie. Susan barked at the staff, rewrote the same paragraph twice, and spilled coffee on her new wool suit. She tried to focus but thoughts of Maggie kept intruding.

When Ed came into her office to discuss Maggie's production company, Susan wanted to yell at him. M.J. Carson was the last person she wanted to discuss.

"I've gotten some preliminary interest from folks who have winter homes in Florida. I was at a party up in Heathrow and there was money. Here's some of the names. What do you think? Think Ms. Carson will be interested?"

"Ed, why are you asking me? This is your area of expertise. If you want me to run financial profiles on them, I'll be glad to. Just don't ask me to do a thumbs up or thumbs down." Susan looked at the open file on her desk hoping the conversation was over.

"Look, Susan, can you run these by Ms. Carson's folks and see what their interest is?"

"No. If you want the financials on these people, I need to get started. If not, let me finish reviewing these contracts. I have to overnight them and they will be picked up at three."

Ed perched on the edge of her desk. "You are the damnedest person I work with. You're hard-nosed and focused. You've kept me, and the company, from losing big bucks. I love to see you do that with our clients. And I hate it when you do it to me."

"Thanks, Ed. I'm going to take that as a compliment."

Ed smiled as he spoke. "I made a good decision persuading you to come to work for me. I get the hint. I'm going."

By two thirty, Susan had arranged to overnight the package and was ready to check the names Ed had given her. Susan signed on to her computer and began the research. If people knew how much information was accessible, Susan was sure they would think twice about some of their spending and credit decisions. As she finished her last query at four, she realized she was finally able to concentrate. At that moment her office assistant informed her that M.J. Carson was on the phone. Her safe world was again threatening to disintegrate.

Maggie yawned and stretched, waiting for Susan to answer the phone. Her head pounded, her eyes ached, and conversation was difficult. She'd spent Sunday working with her staff on the upcoming tour. Work was easier than thinking about Susan. Later, pleased with the plans, she celebrated with her staff and the band members, finally falling asleep around four a.m. When she awoke at two in the afternoon, she realized she hadn't called Susan. She was pleased she had gotten through a whole day without thinking about her.

"Susan Hettinger." Susan sounded distant.

The ground shifted. Maggie quickly adjusted. "Hi, beautiful. I'm sorry I didn't call yesterday. I just got busy."

"No problem. Is there something you need?" Susan was not getting any friendlier.

Need? thought Maggie. *I don't need anything or anyone.* She stopped. That was no longer true. When had that changed? "Look, Susan, I'm sorry. I called because I just wanted to hear your voice. I've missed you." Maggie needed to be her most persuasive self. "How about if the kids and I come pick up you, Cady, and your mom, and we go someplace to eat?"

"Thanks, but—"

"And maybe afterward we can rent a video and watch some movies. I really miss you."

"I think my mom has already made plans and—"

"I'll call her and work something out. I'll call you right back." Maggie hung up and dialed Maureen. Whenever her emotions threatened to get out of control, she switched to autopilot. Do, don't think. She didn't want to give Susan a chance to say no. Five minutes later she was again on the phone to Susan. "Your mom invited us for dinner. Want me to pick you up at work? We can ride to your house together."

"Thanks, but I don't…Maggie, we need to talk—"

Maggie interrupted and promised to meet Susan at her office. At five thirty, Maggie and her two children arrived, driven by Maya in one of the rental cars. Susan was grateful that at least no more limos would be pulling up to her house. Maggie had just said hello when she was pulled into Ed's office. The children ran around until they found Susan's office.

"Miss Susan," Beth said, "is Cady at your house?"

Surprised at the question, Susan replied, "Yes, she lives there with me and her grandmother. Why?"

"I wanted to play with her, but I thought she might be with her daddy."

Susan stared at her and tried to imagine where the questioning had come from. Lifting Beth on her lap, she said, "Cady doesn't have a daddy. She lives with me and her grandmother. And you can play with her anytime."

"Me too?" D.J. added.

"Yeah, you too. Come on. Let's get your mom. I'm hungry."

Susan claimed Maggie, telling Ed to make an appointment during working hours. "I need to get these hungry kids fed, and me too." She pulled Maggie out of her chair. "Don't think about it," Susan warned as he started to speak.

"Okay," Ed said. "Ms. Carson, can we get you in tomorrow to talk about some tentative plans? We just need a little more information so that we can put together a presentation and Susan can run the numbers."

Maggie quickly called Paul in Tampa and set up a meeting for nine the next morning.

As they left, Maggie spoke. "Thanks. I tend to get excited about my work. I'm sorry." Maggie ran her hand through Susan's hair as they drove away.

"Mmm. That feels good." Susan leaned into the caress. Her previous anger dissolved with the gentle touching.

Her mother met them at the door with hugs and ordered the kids off to wash hands. "Dinner is ready. Susan, you and Maggie clean up. I don't want dinner getting cold."

Susan led Maggie to the other side of the house. Once they were alone, she felt strong arms encircle her. There was something about Maggie that Susan found irresistible. She wanted to stay angry, but her head was losing the battle with her body.

"Susan, what's the matter?" Without waiting for an answer, Maggie nibbled at Susan's neck, moving from one side to the other.

Susan's knees shook, threatening to send her tumbling to the floor. She abandoned thought and gave in to her body's burning need. She lifted Maggie's face until she captured the warm lips. The kiss became demanding. Susan wanted to call her body a traitor but she couldn't remember why.

Maggie pulled away. "Have I told you how much I've missed you?" Susan shook her head. "I have." As if to prove how much, she again kissed Susan, a kiss filled with promise.

After dinner, they all adjourned to the family room. Susan watched as Maggie rolled on the floor playing with the kids.

There was something childlike and innocent about her. Giggles filled the room as Maggie pretended to be a cat and batted at a ball on the floor. Complaining followed Susan's disruption to put Cady in bed. In thirty minutes, all three kids were clean and tucked into bed. Susan, Maureen, and Maggie talked for another hour before Maureen claimed it was her bed time. As she hugged Maggie, she whispered, "Glad things are working out."

"Me too," Maggie said. After her mother left, Maggie grabbed Susan's hand. "Why don't we take a shower and then go to bed? I've been dreaming all day about you being naked next to me. And"—she paused, lowering her voice—"what I wanted to do."

Susan leaned against the side of the Jacuzzi, allowing Maggie's hands to slowly move down her body. When Maggie reached her feet, she lifted them and held them against her breasts. Susan was in heaven. Maggie tenderly massaged the bottoms of the feet, then slowly worked up the legs. By the time Maggie stroked her thighs, Susan was having trouble breathing. She tried to pull Maggie closer, but Maggie pushed her away.

"Be patient. Enjoy." Maggie's hands drifted slowly to the inside of Susan's thighs and briefly touched her heated center.

Susan wanted more. Instead Maggie traced circles on her hips, thighs, and stomach in ever-widening arcs. Susan groaned, wondering how much longer she could last. All motion stopped. Susan opened her eyes only to be captured by eyes dark with desire as Maggie slowly moved down between her legs. It was enough to ignite a wildfire in Susan. She was floating out of control.

Maggie's hand slid between wet thighs. Her mouth was consuming. Her fingers explored Susan's body. She wanted to feel Susan come. Maggie's own body burned with desire. Maggie sucked on Susan's swollen clit. "God, I want you."

"Maggie," Susan said as she came. For a few moments she leaned against the tub and relished the pleasure coursing through her body. When she was finally able to breathe, Susan said, "I love you." Susan's heart raced as she saw a lopsided smile make its way across Maggie's face. Beautiful warm eyes and that wonderful, miraculous grin again drew her in. Susan let her hand wander until she could bury it in wetness. Maggie's breathing became shallow. Susan wanted to show Maggie how much love she felt. *You must love me,* Susan prayed as she made love to Maggie.

❖

The rest of the week was a mixture of chaos and lovemaking. And little sleep. Susan finally understood why her friends disappeared at the beginning of a new relationship. Maggie was an incredibly responsive lover. And tireless.

On Wednesday, they flew to California for meetings with Maggie's manager. Maggie was surprised at Susan's aggressiveness when it came to business. She knew Susan was bright and knowledgeable, but this was a new side she hadn't seen before. *Another thing to admire*, she thought. Karl was out of his league, she decided, if he thought he could browbeat Susan. Maggie desperately wanted to watch him try. Instead she excused herself and called Maya.

"Where are you?" Maya asked.

"We're in Los Angeles. Did you get my messages?"

"Yeah, I got all of them. Disney has a script they want you to read. They're going to send someone over to have breakfast and discuss it with you. Just give me the date. I've got a studio in Orlando set up for you to redo your track." Maya searched for her notes and read the date off. "Karl is anxious to book more dates. Have you talked to him?"

"Yes, we're at his office now. No more dates. Not until I see how the first month goes. I'll talk to him." She was frustrated at having this same conversation. "What else?"

"One of the Orlando TV stations called, and they want an exclusive interview. I explained you don't give many interviews, and certainly not exclusive—"

"Exclusive! Who the hell do they think they are?"

"Look, M.J., I'm the messenger. Karl thought it was a great idea since you were in Orlando anyway."

"Fuck. Just set it up. And make sure you get a list of the questions beforehand." She hated this part of her public life. Too many misquotes and two many intrusive questions. "And limit the interview to twenty minutes, no matter what Karl says."

"Anything else?"

"I'll talk to Karl. You take care of the other stuff. Stay in touch." Maggie hung up. The door to Karl's office opened and he came out. "How's it going?"

"She's tough, but smart. Definitely a keeper." Karl winked.

"Karl, I just got off the phone with Maya. No more dates until we've been out on tour for at least a month. And the interview in Orlando—twenty minutes fixed format with questions submitted beforehand, or no interview."

"Christ, M.J., the station needs lots of tape to edit. They're not going to like it."

"Twenty minutes. I want the questions at least three days before."

Karl took a deep breath. "Done. You know you were less demanding ten years ago."

"Ten years ago I was lucky if I got an interview once a year even when I sat in the newspaper's office." In the last ten years she had lost her privacy and resented it.

"I'm impressed," Maggie said as they headed back to the airport. "I've never seen Karl back down from anyone. How did you get him to change that schedule?"

"He's driven by money," Susan said, still feeling the adrenaline flowing.

"Susan, he's also very loyal. Yeah, he's got his prickly side, but he's never, and I repeat, never, betrayed me. He's worth the money."

Once on the plane, Maggie quickly fell asleep, leaving Susan to question interfering in her business. After all, she reminded herself, she was just a bean counter. Maggie had never said anything that indicated she was more than a friend with benefits.

They arrived back in Orlando around midnight. After her in-flight nap, Maggie was rested and aroused. Susan was exhausted and frustrated. She still didn't understand her role in Maggie's life. When they got to the house, Susan reminded Maggie they had an early meeting and then crawled into bed. By the time Maggie had showered, Susan was fast asleep.

On the second trip to California, Maggie gathered her staff together to discuss the upcoming tour while Susan met with potential investors Ed had lined up. During the afternoon they went over various accounts with Karl and his staff. Still energized, Maggie took Susan to her favorite woman's bar, where they danced until two. Several women greeted her when they arrived.

"Are you a regular in this place?" Susan asked.

"I've been here a few times, but two of the women we just talked to have worked on some of my West Coast concerts. You're not jealous, are you?"

Susan's emotions were all over the place. "Should I be?"

"Not on my account." Maggie's face lit up. "Do you want to be jealous? Should I do something to make you jealous?"

Susan stiffened. "I don't do jealous. I'm simply asking a question."

Maggie stopped dancing and led Susan back to the table.

"Susan, you have nothing to worry about." She rubbed the palm of Susan's hand with her thumb and waited for an answer. Maggie's expression was hopeful but Susan remained silent. "Come on, it's late. I'll call the pilot and tell him to have the plane ready."

After take-off, Maggie again fell asleep as they flew to New York. While in the city, they checked out three recording studios and spent time with more investors. By seven that night they were headed back to Florida.

"I guess this is called life in the fast lane," Susan said as she boarded the plane. Her life was spinning out of control, caught in a whirlwind with Maggie as the vortex.

During the following week Susan, Ed, and Maggie spent endless hours discussing details of the proposed production company and the amortization of costs. Maggie's business acumen continued to surprise Susan.

"So you're telling me that because this is considered a high-risk venture, the backers get a higher rate of interest on the money they loan?" Maggie asked.

"They also realize there is no guarantee on their investment."

"I'm no fucking fly-by-night sensation. Everything I have recorded in the last eight years has been solid. This is usury."

"That's why we're trying to set up your own production company," Ed reminded her. "But we have to get backers for the initial startup."

"Why can't Derek and I put up the money?"

"You can," Susan said, "but you're talking about tying up a significant part of your assets for an indeterminate period of time. If you commit too much, you could lose everything. Observing your lifestyle, including these planes we've been chartering, you've got high fixed expenses and you spend freely."

Maggie glared at Susan. "Are you criticizing my life?"

"No, I'm just making an observation."

"What about you? You were traveling first class when we met. There are cheaper ways to travel."

Susan fought for calm. "My house is paid for. My car and furniture are paid for. We have a 401K at work and Ed gives me substantial bonuses, most of which I invest. The first-class tickets are charged to whatever project we're working on. Any more questions?"

Maggie left the room in frustration but returned twenty minutes later. This time the questions were detailed.

The next two days were spent in a studio in Orlando while Maggie finished up a track on her new CD. After the recording sessions were done, Maggie and Susan were flying to Nashville, New York, and California, still looking at recording studios and asking questions. Any time Maggie and Susan were alone was spent in passionate lovemaking.

Ed continued contacting investors and writing the business plan. As a result of the tie with M.J. Carson, two more clients were referred to the firm. Business was booming.

Susan, however, was exhausted. "And I used to think my life was boring, ordinary. I just want my own bed."

On Sunday, Susan slept late but still was up before Maggie. It was hard to leave her lying there asleep, but Susan wanted some quiet time, maybe even time with her family. As she approached the kitchen, she gave up on quiet. Cady, Beth, and D.J. were sitting at the table in the midst of a rather loud song that her mother was teaching them. Susan hesitated before entering, knowing some of the songs her mother knew were definitely R-rated.

As soon as she entered the kitchen, Cady ran up. "Mommy!" Susan hugged her and joined the others at the table. Susan suddenly realized how much of her quiet life she missed.

"Good morning. Want some coffee?" Her mother placed a cup on the table. "Breakfast is almost ready. What time did you get in last night?"

"Around eleven. Our plane was delayed."

"We were talking about going to the mall and doing some Christmas shopping. Would you like to come along?"

"That sounds like a great idea." Susan was pleased at some normalcy. That feeling ended when she returned to her bedroom. Maggie was still asleep, but parts of her body were exposed. Susan couldn't believe how quickly she was aroused.

"Hey, sleepy."

"Mmm. What time is it? How long have you been up?"

"Since eight. Mom, the kids, and I had breakfast and we chatted and then I read the paper. Guess what? You were in the entertainment section."

Chapter Thirteen

Maggie stared up at Susan. *God, she's beautiful. I can't believe how fucking happy I am.* Grinning, she sat up and only briefly wondered what was in the paper. "Any reports that I have been seen with a beautiful woman are true." She playfully pulled Susan onto the bed, quickly covering her with kisses. Her heart was full.

"You are insatiable." Susan laughed. Kisses trailing down her neck distracted but did not deter her. "Mmm, I didn't know you'd made a movie."

"God, Susan, do you know how sexy…" Susan's words finally pierced the wall of sexual arousal Maggie felt building. Just as quickly the wall tumbled. Maggie began rummaging through her luggage for her appointment book. "Oh, fuck. Damn, damn, damn. Where the hell is that PDA?"

Susan stared in amazement as a naked and agitated Maggie threw clothes, shoes, and other objects into the air. "Maggie, we need to work on your vocabulary."

"Oh, shit." Maggie pulled the PDA out of the depths of clothes. "Fuck! I'm sorry." She again began digging through her luggage, this time pulling out clothes. "We've been so busy. I'd forgotten. I know, how could I forget?" Maggie looked at Susan then groaned. "God, you're beautiful. How would you like to go to L.A. tomorrow night?" Without waiting for an answer, Maggie rushed over to Susan and began kissing her.

"Stop! Los Angeles? I can't." Susan pulled away. "Maggie, stop!"

Maggie sat naked in the bed, pouting.

Susan started again. "What about the movie?"

"I'm sorry. I rely on Maya to make sure I don't miss appointments. I haven't talked to her in the last couple of days. The movie opens day after tomorrow. The studio wants it out before the end of the year so it will be eligible for this year's awards. I finished it so long ago I'd forgotten."

Susan stared incredulously. "Awards? Movie? How can you forget something this big?"

"To be honest, we've been kinda busy." The blush creeping up Susan's neck caused Maggie to smile. "Do you know how wonderful you are?" She kissed Susan's eyes and nose. "Karl left a message a month ago about the opening. He thinks I've a good shot at a nomination. But it needs to get exposure in the New York and California markets. We're doing a media blitz over the holidays and into the first of the year. This," Maggie paused for effect, "is the official end of my vacation."

Susan didn't know how to respond. "An Academy Award nomination?" Susan sputtered. "How can you forget you made a movie that may earn you an Oscar?"

"To be honest, I did it last year. If Maya and Karl hadn't reminded me, I wouldn't know what you were talking about."

"I don't understand."

Maggie smiled. "Don't try to. Karl sent me the script and arranged the screen test. The studio and the director were impressed, but it took time to arrange the financing. We shot the movie and it took a while to edit and get it ready for distribution. Now, will you go? I really want you there." To emphasize her point, Maggie began caressing Susan's back and ass. "I really do want you there."

"Won't it be awkward? How are you going to justify my presence?"

Maggie hesitated. "It's okay. No one will think anything. You can be Paul's date. No one will suspect."

"Paul's date? What do you mean no one will suspect?"

"There has been speculation about Paul and Derek, and me, but nothing concrete. Look, I want you to be there for me." For the first time, she was intentionally mixing the personal and professional parts of her life, and she didn't want to think about the possible consequences.

"Come on, Maggie. Are you trying to tell me no one has suspected the truth? People in Atlanta were asking questions, and we weren't that discreet. I know there have been other women." Susan paused, hoping for a refusal, but continued when Maggie was silent. "People can't be that naïve."

"Susan, people believe what they want. You'd be surprised at how many people are still in the closet. Sure, there are suspicions but nothing, and I mean nothing, has ever been confirmed. My staff's worked hard to make sure there aren't any rumors that would impact either one of our careers. I've been careful to not change that image. What's wrong with that?"

"Nothing. Except you're living a lie and constantly afraid someone will find out. Is this the way you and Derek want to live? Well, I don't. I can't." She walked to the door. "For most of my life, I thought I needed to live up to others' expectations. I didn't want to hurt my parents, so I hung around with a group of friends in high school. In college I finally met a woman I loved but she wanted to tell her parents and my parents about us and I said no. She finally left. I married Cady's father because I thought it was safer. Right! As soon as he found out I was pregnant, he walked. I tried to be someone I wasn't, and I was miserable. I can't live that way." She couldn't separate her anger with Maggie from her own struggles with coming out. These were the same arguments she had once used years ago. "I won't."

"Damn it, Susan, what do you want me to do? Plead mea culpa? Fuck it, I've worked hard. What more do you want me to do?"

"Aren't you famous enough?"

"What difference does that make? If you don't toe the line, if you don't fit the image, the industry kills you. I have been singing and playing clubs and one-night gigs since I was sixteen. Now I'm a fucking overnight whiz. I don't want to start over."

"So you want to live a lie so you can be rich and famous?"

"No, I just want to live. What are we supposed to do? When people like Pat Robertson call for a holy war on perverts—that's you and me, Susan—what do I do? Give some religious zealot a license to shoot me and the people I care about and give them a damn map to make it easier to find my house? I'm not going to do it. I'm a public figure. I don't like it, but that's part of the price of success. I have enough problems with crazy fans who like me. I am not putting myself and my loved ones in harm's way. I won't let anything, or anyone, harm them. And that includes you."

The vehemence of Maggie's protest caused Susan to back up emotionally. "I'm not asking you to out anyone. It was a mistake for me to marry Cady's dad. When Tom left, my boss told me he was surprised I'd gotten married. You know why? He thought I was gay. I won't go back."

Maggie tried to find some common ground. "I'm not asking you to, Susan. It's not just me, though. What about Derek? How do you think being outed will play in the locker room? Do you think some tough, macho football player is going to like sharing a shower with him? I don't want him hurt, emotionally or physically. Especially with such little time left in the season." Maggie wanted an end to this conversation. "Please, a little longer and it won't make a difference. Derek's retiring at the end of the season and then it won't matter as much." Susan didn't respond. "Look, just this one thing, okay? Please." In spite of her fear, Maggie wanted Susan in her life. "Do you want me to beg? I will. Please."

"I have worked hard to get my life together. Coming out was difficult and I won't go back. I can't."

Maggie sighed. "I understand. I'm not asking you to. And I won't ask you to lie." Maggie had lied so much about so many things, she knew truth was difficult. And most of the time she wasn't sure what was true. She was tired of the deceit, but she wasn't sure how to change. "I really want you there."

"Maggie, I don't know. I need to do some Christmas shopping. Cady and Mom have been troupers...My life has gone to hell, Maggie, and I want some part of it back."

Maggie had no idea what Susan meant, but the look on her face was enough. "What can I do? What do you want?"

"I want some time to spend with Cady and Mom. I want quiet. I've got work that has been left hanging. I want my life the way it was."

"Let's bring your mom and Cady with us. We have a huge house. My kids would love being home for a few days. You can use my office and my staff will help any way they can." Maggie went in search of Maureen. "How would you like to go to L.A. for a few days? A movie I made is opening, and we'll all go to the premiere."

"Movie! Absolutely. I can't wait to tell the girls at my book club." Maureen danced out of the room. Maggie laughed and returned to find Susan.

Recognizing the effort Maggie was making, Susan gave in. "I need to get some work done."

"Not a problem."

Once in California, neither Susan nor her mother were prepared for the size of the estate. "Good grief," Susan gasped. "This is bigger than my high school. Do you provide maps?"

"Mommy, is this a castle?" Cady asked.

"I don't know, Cady. The only castle I have ever seen was at Disney World."

"Come on, let me show you around. It really isn't that big," Maggie said. For the first time, she began to look at her house through an outsider's eyes. She was excited when they bought the place, especially with its intact recording studio. Derek installed a gym in another area of the house. She never thought of it as ostentatious, glittery, or any of the other words she associated with success. It was home. Now she realized how she had fallen into the same mold as many other Californians. Bigger is better. She wondered how it had happened.

The house was magnificent. Susan recalled touring the Biltmore in Ashville, but this was the first time she'd been in something that someone actually lived in. Even her mother stared in awe.

After a quick tour, Maggie, Susan, and Maureen headed out to buy evening clothes. The next twenty-four hours were a blur. Someone arranged a cocktail party. Maggie and Derek walked around the room greeting people. Maggie was quick to introduce Susan and her mother as their guests. Her mother joined in the festivities as if it were an everyday event.

Susan, however, felt out of place trying to maintain idle chatter with strangers. They were recognizable strangers for the most part. Maggie stopped every few minutes to check on her but then was off again to schmooze with the glitterati. The three-hour time difference between the two coasts finally wore Susan down.

Maya pulled Susan aside. "Come on, I'll take you to a nice quiet place where you can get some sleep."

"I need to let Maggie know."

"Don't worry. I'll tell her. Besides, these things usually go really late."

Maya led her down a series of halls and finally up the stairs. Susan wondered if it was too late to drop breadcrumbs, but she was too tired to search for any. When she finally reached her bedroom, she climbed into bed and was soon fast asleep.

Strange dreams haunted her sleep, and in the morning she was still exhausted. Struggling awake, she dressed and managed to find her mother in the kitchen talking to one of the cooks. Susan grabbed some coffee and sat and listened to the conversation. Her respite from chaos ended when Maggie entered the room.

"What happened to you? Where have you been?" Maggie slipped her arms around Susan and nuzzled her neck. "I missed you," she said. "Maureen, would you mind if I borrow your daughter? I assure you my intentions are entirely dishonorable."

Her mother laughed and nodded, much to Susan's chagrin.

For the next three hours, Maggie showed no signs of fatigue. Susan again found herself easily aroused by Maggie and reveled in the passionate depths they explored. Only the alarm going off at eleven halted the lovemaking.

"Who committed us to this insane opening tonight? God, I don't want to get up." Maggie's hand lazily roamed up and down Susan's thigh.

Susan watched Maggie's hand and realized how easy it was to love her. Her enthusiasm, her passion, her childlike curiosity, her talent. Her tenderness, her kindness, her attentiveness. *Yet I have never heard her say she loves me. Nor has she ever talked about the future. Our future.*

After lunch, the adults adjourned to dress for the big premiere. In high school, Susan once took forty-five minutes to get ready for a date. This particular afternoon was in another league. There were people who specialized in every part of the body. She compared herself to the Tin Man, with mechanics working on every inch. Her mother was thrilled with the attention, but Susan was more bewildered. By evening, they were coifed, painted, dressed, and bejeweled.

Susan stared at herself in the mirror, not sure who that woman was. The image was a sophisticated creature unafraid of anything. Diamonds dangled from her ears, surrounded her neck, and even glittered in her hair. The soft, flowing white designer dress adorned a body totally unfamiliar. This woman was beautiful.

Her mother walked into the room and Susan realized how her mother must have enchanted her father. The young, beautiful, redheaded Maureen, full of life and mischief, was easily recognizable, even after all these years. For the first time Susan wished she was more like her mom.

Susan walked out to where everyone was gathering. When she saw Maggie, she stopped, unable to move. Maggie was stunning dressed in a beautiful long, red, low-cut evening dress with a sexy slit up one side. Susan had trouble breathing. She desperately wanted to make love to her, but she wasn't sure how to get out of her own dress. "You're gorgeous. I just realized I've never seen you in a dress, and you are beautiful."

Maggie laughed. "Thank you. Don't get too excited. I don't really do dresses. You, however, were made for that gown." She swallowed hard. "You take my breath away."

"Thank you. You make me feel beautiful."

At five thirty, the limousine arrived to take them to the party. First cocktails, then the movie, then the after-movie party. As she walked into the theater, Susan was handed a pen and a piece of paper. Seeing the panic on Susan's face, Maggie laughed and quickly grabbed the items and signed them. Once inside Susan looked around and realized this was Ed's dream—to be in a group like this. If he were here, he'd be working this room and have half a dozen phone numbers and appointments by now. Several recognizable people wandered around chatting with other glamorous people. Maggie and Derek were greeted by everyone.

While Derek and Maggie worked the room, Paul escorted Maureen and Susan to a bar and offered each a glass of wine. "Stick to this. It's safer than most of these exotic drinks you'll find around here." He took Susan's hand and pointed out various people. In the presence of such luminaries, Susan was awestruck.

"Maggie's agent is good at arranging these things." Paul smiled behind his wineglass. "Half the people here have never met Maggie, and many of the males are more interested in meeting Derek and talking football, especially with the Raiders playing so well."

"How do you stand this? Look at my mom. She acts like she knows these people."

"Your mom is a charmer, Susan. They probably think she is somebody or has connections. And even if she doesn't, she is enchanting. After this season, Derek is planning on a much simpler life. He's had enough."

The lights dimmed and everyone entered the theater. Her mother, firmly ensconced in the middle of the group, leaned over to speak to Susan. "I can't believe we're here. I'm so excited."

"Me too, Mom." Susan squeezed her mother's hand as the movie began. Maggie was quite good. Susan wondered if there was anything she couldn't do. As Susan observed the familiar head tilt as Maggie talked to her on-screen mother, Susan wanted to reach over and touch her.

The movie ended to great applause. Derek hugged Maggie. "Mags, I am so proud of you. It's every bit as good as Karl said it was." He kissed her cheek as Maggie beamed. For a moment Susan felt very alone.

Paul grabbed Susan and her mother. "Come on. That was the easy part. Now we schmooze and wait for the early reviews. And if you two lovely women are lucky, we'll actually get something to eat." He deftly led them out of the crowd and to the waiting limousine. Fifteen minutes later Maggie and Derek finally climbed in.

The rest of the evening was another Maggie tornado. First cocktails, then a late dinner at some fancy, well-known restaurant where they were soon surrounded by a supportive crowd. Then dessert, coffee, more cocktails, and more talking. People wished Maggie, the producer, the director, and anyone else good luck, offered comments about the movie, or just stopped to gossip.

"M.J., this will be a hit." Maggie's agent was jumping in and out of his chair greeting people. "We'll set up Leno and some other West Coast interviews, then go to New York and do Letterman and the *Today* show. How about it? I've got to make some calls in the morning, but I can confirm a few more."

Maggie sipped her drink and greeted another well-wisher. Alone for a moment, she turned to Karl, "I don't want to fly back and forth. Tell me again why I'm doing this?"

"M.J., you agreed to promote the movie when we signed the contract to do it. It's great for you and the movie."

"You know I hate talking to people. Derek, I'm nervous."

"Mags, you'll do fine," Derek said. "You and Susan go."

She crossed her arms. "I've gone to all your NFL awards banquets, your team parties, and the team family get-togethers. Why can't you go with me?"

"You're perfectly capable of handling this. And, no, you haven't been to all my awards banquets. Nice try. How many times have you been on the road or had a conflict? Especially of the female gender." Maggie couldn't deny his accusations.

Watching them, Susan wondered again how she fit into their life. More unanswered questions. Finally fatigue kicked in. Her mom's yawning gave Susan an excuse. "Paul, can you take Mom and me back to Maggie's? We're both tired."

"Susan, please stay," Maggie said. "We can send your mom home in the limo or Paul could go with her. Please stay."

Susan was tired. The swirl of emotions had depleted her reserve. She desperately needed some sleep. "We'll see you later. Good night, Derek."

As Susan and Maureen left with Paul, Maggie's emotions were tumultuous. She wanted Susan to stay and was afraid she would.

"Mags," Derek said, "there's a reporter here from the NBC affiliate. He's coming over to talk to us." Derek pointed to a smiling, young attractive man headed their way. "He's been at the practice field asking questions."

Maggie nodded and sighed. "I hate talking to the press. Urrrrgh." As the reporter reached her, Maggie turned on the charm but waited for him to begin the questioning.

"Ms. Carson, my name's Randy Beaman. I'm a reporter with KMBC. Your movie performance is amazing, especially for a newcomer."

"Thank you. I take that as a compliment." Maggie spoke in a friendly voice, controlling the seething desire to strangle the pest. *Newcomer!* she thought. *You haven't done your homework.* "I was fortunate to have a good script and an excellent director and costar." *And I worked fourteen to eighteen hours each day.*

"Our station would like to get you in for an interview." The young reporter spoke with certainty, clearly confident M.J. Carson would not turn him down.

Maggie wanted to smack the smug prick, but she spoke calmly. "Mr. Beaman, I can't imagine what you could find interesting about me. Thank you so much for the offer. If you still insist on talking to a novice like me, that's Karl, my manager." Maggie pointed to the corner where Karl held court. "Set it up with him. Excuse me, but I want to thank my director. Derek, have I introduced you to Mr. Walden?" Grabbing his arm, she walked off. "Asshole," Maggie muttered only loud enough for Derek to hear. "Newcomer, right!"

"Come on," Derek said, "forget him. Thinks he's the next Hemingway."

"I've always loved your sense of humor. Come on, let me introduce you to my director." After introducing Derek to the director, Maggie wandered off and found Maya. "Did you pick up the packages?"

"Yeah, I've got them in the car. Do you want them now? I wasn't sure if you wanted to wear them tonight or not, so I brought both packages. Do you want them now?"

"Just give them to me before the reviews come out."

"I can drop them off tomorrow," Maya said.

"No! I want them tonight."

Maya went and retrieved the packages. Maggie smiled when she thought about surprising Susan. For the first time in her life, she'd thoroughly enjoyed shopping. She wanted to give Susan something to show her how much she cared about her. It was exciting to pick something so personal. Maggie grinned, imaging Susan's reaction to the surprise.

During the drive back to Maggie's, Susan allowed her imagination and fears to slowly take control. When she failed to pay attention to the conversation in the limo, she attributed it to her physical state. "I'm just tired. I just need some sleep."

As they entered the house, Paul asked, "Susan, is something wrong?"

"It's...nothing." Tears threatened. Susan looked up at him. "How do you do this? Go to these parties and pretend to be just another hanger-on."

"I know this is business for them. When the lights and crowd are gone, I know what I have. That's all I need."

"That's fine, but I don't know what she wants."

"I've not known Maggie very long, but I know that you're important to her. In the four years since I met her, you're the first person she has spent any time with and who's actually met her family. I also know that she often doesn't know what she wants and sometimes gets caught up in her own P.R. Then her insecurities take control. When that happens, she just has difficulty letting people know that she cares." Paul gave her a brief hug and went to his room.

Susan quietly walked with her mother. When they reached Maureen's room, Susan stopped.

"Do you want to talk?" Maureen asked.

Susan had always appreciated her mother's concern. This time she wasn't sure if talking to her mother would help. "I'm fine, Mom. Just tired."

"Maggie loves you. I have no doubt about that."

"How can you be so sure?"

Her mother had no trouble answering, "Honey, all you have to do is see how she looks at you to know how she feels. And when I see the two of you together, I know it will work. Be patient. True love is worth it."

"I didn't know you were such a romantic."

"Talk to her, Susan." Maureen brushed the hair on Susan's forehead. "If we're lucky, we'll have one great love in our lives. Someone who will make us feel weak in the knees and laugh with us. And if we're blessed with that kind of love, we may have to work to keep it."

Susan stared at her mom. She kissed her cheek, said good night, then stumbled into bed. As she closed her eyes, she acknowledged that Maggie did make her feel weak in the knees and totally out of control. One question nagged her as she fell asleep: *Why can't she tell me if she loves me?*

Warm breaths trailing down Susan's back gently drew her from sleep. Without opening her eyes, Susan rolled onto her back. As fingers danced across her stomach, she recognized the nascent arousal. She opened her eyes and found herself staring up into Maggie's smiling face.

"Hi, gorgeous." Maggie placed a box filled with long stem roses on Susan's chest. "Guess what? They love it. Every one of the reviews was glowing." She traced kisses down Susan's cheek, neck, and shoulders. "Here. These are for you. I just wanted to say thank you for being here with me."

Susan sat up and opened the box of roses. On top was a smaller box. Childlike joy danced across Maggie's face. Susan slowly opened the smaller box. Inside was a pair of beautiful diamond earrings. They were at least a carat each and expensive.

"Do you like them?" When Susan nodded, Maggie was thrilled. "Good, because there's another box in there with something that matches." Impatient with Susan's slow searching, she pulled the second small box out. She opened it to reveal a diamond solitaire ring.

"Maggie, I can't. This is too much."

"Yes, you can. Try it on and I'll get it sized if it doesn't fit. I tried one of yours on and kind of judged the size from that." Maggie lifted the ring out of the box and nervously played with it. Her expression became serious. "I wanted some way to tell you how I feel. For the first time, I think about things I want to do for us." Maggie slid the ring on Susan's left hand. "Do you know how good that feels? To have an us?" She played with the ring as she spoke. "I want you to wear this, so that no matter where I am or what I am doing, you can think of me and I will be a part of you. I want you to know how much you mean to me."

This unexpected expression of feeling touched something deep inside Susan. A place no one else had ever come near. Maggie took Susan into her arms and murmured lists of things she adored about her. Susan relaxed into the embrace. Still she questioned what she was hearing. *With all the women she can have, why me?* Before she could come up with an answer, Susan's body demanded attention. Her breathing became rapid and a moan slipped out.

"I want to make mad, passionate love for the next three days."

"I thought you had dates with Katie, Dave, and Jay." Susan

found talking difficult. "Aren't they going to occupy your time this week?"

"M-m-m-m! You taste wonderful"

Susan tried one more time before she lost all sense of anything except Maggie's hands and lips. "What about your interviews?"

"Damn, you are the most persistent person." Maggie laughed. "You are incredible. Okay, we're staying here until the day after tomorrow and I'll do two interviews and Leno tomorrow, then we head for New York. Interviews for two days and then back to Orlando by Friday. I promise. Okay?"

Susan nodded but she doubted if she would remember what was said. She was caught in a tornado and knew it was not the time to discuss the changing wind direction. Heated kisses erased all thoughts but the feeling of Maggie's lips. Her lips and hands caressed, teased, and played. Susan's body might have been exhausted but her libido was just awakening. Her body was on fire. Maggie's fingers brushed against the inside of Susan's thigh. Susan was losing control. She pushed the hand closer to her center, wanting relief.

Susan cried out as she let go. Her arms tightly around Maggie, she whispered, "Mags, I love you. I love you."

CHAPTER FOURTEEN

Maggie prepared for the interviews, her mood dark. Karl and Maya had arrived before noon to brief her. Her hair stylist and make-up people arrived in time to ready her for *The Tonight Show*. Still her nervousness wore on the rest of her staff. She knew this was part of the fame, but she still didn't like it.

"M.J., will you sit down?" Maya put the notes in front of Maggie for one last review. "Sometimes I can't believe you were an English major."

"Majoring in English doesn't automatically assure you of being a competent public speaker. I majored in English because I liked to read and write, neither of which require communicating orally with another person." Maggie picked up the notes, read them, and put them back down. "Where's Susan? Did you know I hate public speaking?"

"She and her mom are shopping. I suggested it."

"What for? Why didn't you consult me?"

"You need to concentrate," Karl added, "and she interferes. Besides, you need to cool it with her. You're going to be under close scrutiny and you can't afford a scandal."

"No, you cool it, Karl. Susan is part of my life."

"M.J., we're doing our job and protecting you," Karl said. "You don't need this affair getting—"

"Stop! Susan is off-limits. To you, Maya, and anyone else. I will not give her up. Do you understand?"

Karl nodded and quickly changed the subject. "After these interviews are over, why don't you take some time off? We can get that place up near Yosemite that you like so much."

Maggie glared. "Don't handle me, Karl. I'll decide where and when I want to go if I decide to take time off." Maggie was tired. She mentally promised to take time off in New York to shop with Susan.

❖

In New York, Maggie had five interviews with print media, three with electronic media, two phone interviews, and a photo shoot. Susan was frustrated and wondered why she'd even bothered with this trip. She shopped alone. By the time they arrived in Orlando it was almost Saturday.

Susan felt guilty. She had promised to be home early enough to spend some time with her family. She tried to get into the house quietly. In the past, Susan had relaxed after a trip by spending a few moments with her mother before going to sleep, but Maggie wanted to play.

"Why don't you go ahead and go to bed? I'll be in shortly."

"I can wait on you." Maggie ran her hands across Susan's breasts. "But I may not be able to wait long."

Susan stopped Maggie's roaming hands. "Please. I just need a few minutes. I don't know how you keep going. I just need some time for me."

"Fine!" Maggie stormed off without another word.

Susan wanted Maggie to go away so she could wake up her mom and just talk. She didn't mean to make Maggie angry. She just wanted some quiet. Her life was again filled with conflict.

The next morning Susan and Maggie rode in silence out to the airport to meet Maggie's kids and Maya. Maggie was still pouting because Susan refused to go to bed when she did.

At the airport, Maggie was recognized and stopped for autographs. A crowd formed, jostling and shoving to get closer. The noise and the pushing frightened Cady. Susan picked Cady up and walked away, calling out that she would wait in the car.

"Mom, are those people trying to hurt Miss Maggie?"

"No, sweetheart, they just want to talk to her and get her autograph."

"What's aulo gaff?"

"It's autograph, sweetie. That is when people sign their names. When you write your name, that's your autograph."

"I don't want to learn to write." Cady's face had a serious look.

"I write my name all the time, and no one asks for my autograph." Susan wanted to reassure her, but she was not able to convince herself. "You'll be a very good writer, and I promise you will always be safe." Would they ever have any privacy again?

Confused by Susan's sudden disappearance, Maggie gathered her children and the luggage. The media showing up infuriated her. She had no doubts Karl was behind it.

As the crowd closed in, Maggie spoke to Maya. "Hold on to the kids. Head to the door. Susan will probably be right outside."

Susan circled the terminal while watching for Maggie. A large, noisy crowd burst from the doorway like water too long held behind an earthen dam. At the head of the frantic flow was Maggie, Maya, and two children. Susan quickly pulled up to the entrance and pushed the button to open the side doors of the minivan. The cresting crowd followed. Somehow, everyone managed to get into the van before the swarm reached them.

❖

By the time they reached Winter Park, Maggie wanted to shake Susan and ask what the hell was wrong. When they were finally alone at bedtime, she asked, "What's going on? You've hardly talked to me all day."

"I'm tired, Mags. Can we just let it rest?"

"What happened between going to the airport and coming back from the airport?"

"You." The answer stunned Maggie. She sat on the edge of the bed while Susan rummaged in a dresser for a pair of socks. "Your need for attention. All those people at the airport. I don't like losing my life, or interrupting my daughter's. And your damned need to hide."

"Susan, do you understand now why I protect my privacy?"

"If you're going to compare today's episode with your hiding your sexual orientation, it won't work." Susan crossed the room, pacing like an animal stalking its prey.

"I'm talking about privacy," Maggie spat out. "You've just gotten a small taste of what my life is like, and you don't like it. Well, guess what? I don't either. I didn't arrange today. And when I find out who did, I'll make sure it doesn't happen again. I want to keep my kids safe and away from the public. I'm sorry about Cady. I don't want her, or you, or your mother to have to go through this. Right now there isn't a damn thing I can do to stop it except be discreet. And control the information people have."

"I love you, Maggie, and I don't want to hide. I also want more order in my life."

"I do too, sweetheart," Maggie sighed. "I do too."

CHAPTER FIFTEEN

When Maggie needed to return to California, she pleaded with Susan to fly with her. "It's only for a couple of days. There's some problem with the tour and Karl wants me back there."

"I've been traveling so much that I'm getting behind at work. Besides, I need to do my Christmas shopping. Maggie, you promised to go shopping with me in New York and we didn't. You promised we would have some time in Florida. We've been here four days and now you want to get on another damn airplane. I need to get caught up at work. I'm getting too far behind in everything. I need to spend some time here." *What I really need,* Susan thought, *is quiet.*

"It's only for a couple of days."

"No, Maggie, you have a lot of things to take care of and I have a lot of things to take care of. You'll be lucky to get everything taken care of in a week. I'm staying here."

Maggie kept trying up until she left for the airport, but Susan was adamant. She was staying in Florida. She arrived at work early, unlocked the door to the office, stepped in, and closed her eyes. Silence. From the soles of her shoes to the soul of her body, she inhaled the peace and sanity.

Fifteen minutes later Ed arrived and was pleasantly surprised to find her in the office. "Well, how goes it? I've got to tell you, the phone has not stopped ringing in the last week. Most of it's routine business. But for the first time, I have people trying to get my home phone number. The staff has been good at not giving your or my phone number out. Although they've had some great—"

"What about my phone number?"

Susan's stomach began an unearthly dance. Ed turned serious. "Susan, there are some media people trying to track you down. Somehow they have identified you as Ms. Carson's traveling companion. They want to know more about you and your relationship. Right now, I think they want to know if you are an agent and can set up an interview."

"How did they get my name and where I worked?" Susan's blood pressure was rising faster than her breakfast.

"I don't know. Someone called looking for the woman accompanying M.J. Carson. I haven't asked any questions. It's not any of my business." Ed hesitated. "Is there something you want to talk about?"

Susan didn't want to lie but she wasn't sure how to explain about her relationship with Maggie. "Ed, I'm sorry if I—"

"Don't apologize. I feel like I let my greed get in the way."

"Ed, no…" Susan was unable to finish her thought.

"Let me take some of the responsibility. Take some time off if you need to."

"Not yet. There would be twice as much to do."

By nine, all the staff had arrived and appeared to be in a much more subdued mood. Susan sensed a polite distance every time anyone but Ed came into her office. By noon, she was ready to scream.

At lunch, she cornered Ed. "If your earlier offer still stands, I need to talk." He nodded. Susan felt like a teenager explaining to her mom why she had stayed out late with a date. "Ed, I apologize if I've let you down or put the office in an uncomfortable spot. I am…I have… How do I say this?"

"Maybe I can help. Is there something going on between you and M.J. Carson?"

"It just happened. I can take leave if you want me to." Susan couldn't look at Ed. She had never allowed her personal life to mix with her professional. She ran her fingers over the linen in her jacket sleeve. "Life has become complicated, and it looks like it's affecting work."

"I suspected something was going on. I noticed the way she looked at you when we went to lunch, the way she talks about you. But she was married. Stereotyping, I guess."

"I thought the same thing. It's complicated."

"I won't say anything. I owe you an apology. I'll reassign Ms. Carson if you want, but I don't have anyone with your abilities. While I'm thrilled about having Carson as a client, you are more important to me. I don't want you hurt."

"Ed…" Susan paused to regain her composure. "I…Thank you. Right now, what I need help with most is the office staff." They discussed the problem and decided directness was the best possible solution, especially with the close working relationships of all the staff.

A hastily arranged meeting drew all the staff into the large conference room. The group was unusually somber.

Ed spoke. "As you know, Susan has been out of the office quite a bit in the last few weeks. She has been the guest of M.J. Carson and her family. As you are also aware, we have gotten several new clients recently, partially as a result of M.J. Carson's agreement with this firm. There have also been phone calls and some questions. We must, at all costs, respect our clients' privacy. Susan, however, has agreed to answer any questions as long as it doesn't violate Ms. Carson's privacy."

The room was silent as each person waited for someone else to ask the questions they had gossiped about all week. Finally, Carla, one of Susan's financial assistants, raised her hand and hesitantly asked, "Is Harrison Ford as good looking in person? I heard he was at some party you went to."

The ice was broken. The friendly, casual work atmosphere returned, but Susan recognized she was now viewed as having some stellar status. She was more than just the bean pusher. Susan accepted the changes with mixed emotions.

❖

Maggie faithfully called every evening. Karl had arranged more interviews and publicity events for the movie as well as some pre-tour gigs. The two days lengthened into a week. Susan missed Maggie. One evening as Susan watched Maggie being interviewed on television, she realized how easily the reporter was captivated by M.J. Carson. She knew all too well the sensation. The phone rang, interrupting her thoughts.

"Hi, there," Maggie whispered. "This is an obscene phone call. Hope I have the right number."

Susan smiled and leaned back against her chair. "Boy, do you have my number."

Maggie's laughter was warm and encouraging. Susan imagined her, her head tossed back, eyes filling with tears, and laughter rolling across those wonderful lips.

"I wish I were there right now. I would take you to bed and make you forget everything but me."

In that moment, Susan's life felt empty. Organized, quiet, yes, but empty. "I miss you." The words were out before her brain could edit them.

A short silence floated across endless space. Susan held her breath. "I miss you too. A lot," Maggie said.

Susan felt a spark ignite. *Maggie said I am important in her life.* She fanned that spark into a flame. *She must love me!* The spell was broken when Maggie told a funny story about an interviewer. Susan held on to that thread while she listened to Maggie's tales.

On Friday, the M.J. Carson whirlwind arrived in a rather large caravan of white stretch limousines. With great flourish Maggie persuaded Ed to close the office for the day so she could take everyone to lunch. All afternoon, Maggie played the perfect hostess, and the office staff fell under her spell. They were already in love with her before she announced she had arranged for everyone, and family and significant others, to spend the next day at Disney.

Shortly before five, Maggie had everyone back at the office. Some of the braver souls managed photos and autographs. For once the office was slow to empty on a Friday afternoon. Finally only Ed, Maggie, and Susan were left.

"M.J., you are much too gracious with my staff. They will never want to work again." Ed pulled up a chair. "If you have a few moments, I think I have the financing you're seeking."

By eight that evening Susan was numb, exhausted, and hungry. She tried to duck out of the office but was stopped by Maggie grabbing her arm.

"I'm sorry," Maggie said. "I didn't realize how late it was. Let me take you home, or at least, take you both to dinner."

Ed declined, saying he had plans with his wife. When they were alone, Maggie asked, "And may I see you home?"

"Thanks, but I have my car."

"Then may I ride with you? I have some rather lascivious thoughts I want to share with you." Instant heat traveled up Susan's body. She felt the blushing on her neck and face and she was sure her nipples were erect. She was too embarrassed to look.

"Come on," Maggie said, "let's go home before you have heart palpitations."

After dismissing the limo, they headed toward Winter Park. Her mother had dinner waiting, and while Susan and Maggie finished eating, she put the children to sleep. When she returned to the dining room, she talked with them for a short time before excusing herself and wishing them good night.

"She's not always subtle," Susan said.

An awkward silence followed. As with all silences, there arrived a time when the quiet was deafening and only speaking silenced it. Maggie spoke first. "Well, shall we go to bed?"

Once in the bedroom, Maggie pulled Susan close. "I don't know what's wrong, but if I've done something…"

Susan sensed a hesitancy and something else. She realized this was a part of Maggie she didn't know. She lifted her hand to wipe away a tear.

"Maggie, what's the matter?"

"I don't know. I just missed you. I guess…I don't know." She tried to turn away but Susan reached for her. Maggie grasped her, allowing her defenses to surrender to the love and acceptance she felt from Susan. "I don't have a lot of experience with having a family. My mother died when I was young. My dad, a drunk, was rarely at home. My older brother and sister were left to care for me, but they were trying to find their own escape."

Susan couldn't imagine such a childhood. She stroked Maggie's hair. In spite of the frustration and embarrassment she felt as a teenager with an unconventional mother, Susan always felt love and support. Maggie had gotten quiet. Susan brushed the hair off of Maggie's forehead, wishing there was some way to wipe away the past.

Morning arrived too soon. Susan's dreams were filled with strange shapes and anguished faces. Maggie, however, bounced out, ignoring any attempts to talk about the previous night.

Saturday was a circus, as Maggie's trip to Disney had everyone excited. Even though she'd arranged for the entourage to come through a special entrance and receive preferential treatment, she was often approached by people and asked for autographs. The Disney people made a great effort at providing security, but it was impossible to keep everyone away.

Susan often found herself doing things with her mom and kids while Maggie signed autographs, visited with various Disney cast members, and spoke with various staff. By noon, she was tired of waiting for Maggie and decided to enjoy the rest of the day regardless of Maggie.

That evening Susan and Maggie had their first big argument. "Why didn't you wait for me?" Maggie asked. "All afternoon I kept looking for you."

"How could you possibly miss me with all those adoring fans? I can't believe you even let some stranger ride with us at the Haunted Castle."

"I didn't let him. He jumped in. Where the hell were you? You know this is part of my job. My next picture is with Disney. Why can't you be more cooperative?"

"Because my family and I are not going to be front-page fodder just to further your career. What difference does it make what we do?"

"Susan, what do you want me to do? Hold your hand while we walked around? Disney wouldn't be happy—"

"Don't go there. Disney has a policy of nondiscrimination based on sexual orientation."

"I can't risk my career. Besides, it's good to sign a few—"

"A few! A few hundred. You love being the center of attention. Well, you are not my sun, and I am not a planet to be caught in your solar system."

"I never asked you to be a planet. What I most appreciated is that you were my friend, not some ass-kissing, brown-nose sycophant."

"My God! She does know words with more than four letters."

"Fuck you!"

Susan saw the tears filling Maggie's eyes as Maggie quickly turned away. This was not the way she treated people she cared about. "Maggie, I'm so—"

"Wait!" Maggie said. "I'm sorry. I know I'm being short-tempered. Let's go to bed and get some sleep. I don't have to be anywhere for the next few days. We'll talk tomorrow. Please."

"Maggie, I'm sorry." She reached for her hand. "I do love you. I know I've told you that before. I don't know if you feel the same way or if I'm just the current entertainment."

"Oh, God, Susan. You know me better than that."

"How? How should I know? What do you feel?"

"I…I…I. There was someone a long time ago, but not like this. I…"

"You what?"

"I'm trying to tell you." Maggie ran her hands through her hair. "You are very special." Maggie struggled for the right words, but she wasn't sure what they were.

"What about love? Do you love me? Or am I just a good friend?"

"No. I mean yes. I mean you are more than a friend." What exactly was her relationship with Susan? Maggie had asked herself that question repeatedly. "I guess I haven't really thought about… That doesn't sound good. Let me start again."

"Forget it, Maggie. You have a very neat life and I'm just a complication."

"Please, Susan. Don't walk away. This…this is all new to me. These feelings. I'm trying." What held her back from expressing her feelings? Maggie struggled, but her self-protection was so strong. *Maybe I'll just show her how I feel*, she decided. Smiling, she held out her hand and waited for Susan to take it. Maggie stood quietly waiting, anticipating rejection yet pleading for acceptance.

Susan stared at the long fingers and outstretched palm. Susan's heart and head were again at war. Slowly, Maggie's familiar smile emerged. She knew that Maggie had filled a place in her heart that no one else had even visited. Maggie was waiting with outstretched hand. Susan allowed her heart to answer.

❖

Christmas week was relatively quiet, spent with Susan's sister at her large house on the river near Jacksonville. Susan's family, Derek, Maggie, and their children were all there and filled the two-story structure. Laughter and animated voices were everywhere and time moved too quickly for Susan. As they were preparing to drive back to Orlando after Christmas, Maggie quickly hugged Betsy. "Thank you for sharing Christmas. I don't know when I had a nicer time."

"We all enjoyed having you here, especially my sister." Betsy smiled at Susan. "Travel safely and I'll talk to you soon."

Maggie held Susan's hand as they headed south. "Your family is wonderful. I don't know when I have eaten so much or laughed so hard. The kids had a great time too. I can't believe your brother-in-law talked Derek and Paul into staying another day just to have a guys' day."

"He can't wait to tell everybody he had Derek Baxter at his house. And I'll be glad to have you alone for twenty-four hours before the crowd heads back toward Orlando. Thank you for letting my kids and mom stay longer and come back with Derek and Paul."

"They'll be heading to the hotel with the kids so that they can have some special alone time with the kids. There's plenty of room on Paul's plane. They'll just send Maureen and the kids in the limo to your house." Maggie ran her hand across Susan's leg. "Besides I have my own motives."

There was something salacious about the way Maggie spoke that caused Susan's clit to tingle. "If you don't behave, I won't be able to concentrate on driving and we'll end up in big trouble."

"Mmm. Whips and chains trouble?" Maggie laughed at Susan's wide-eyed expression. "I'm only kidding. I'll behave— until we're alone."

❖

The entire week between Christmas and New Year's was the most peaceful Susan had known since meeting Maggie. She was beginning to feel some semblances of sanity were returning.

Early on New Year's Eve, Susan and Maggie arrived at the Disney hotel in plenty of time to dress for the evening's festivities. Before Christmas, they had decided to postpone opening each other's presents until they were back in Orlando. Susan had fretted over what to get her but had finally found the perfect gift. New Year's Eve they would exchange personal gifts.

Since Maggie was part of the evening entertainment, she left for rehearsal and promised to meet everyone later. Paul and Susan sat in the living area waiting for Derek to finish dressing so they could head for dinner.

"I'm glad I'll have some time with you." Paul smiled. "I don't know what kind of persuasion you have, but I have never seen Maggie so captivated by anyone. You're great for her, Susan. I hope she's telling you how much she appreciates you."

"Paul, I feel like I'm the lucky one. Maggie's smile can light up a room. She can be considerate, gentle, so…passionate." Realizing what she'd said, Susan stopped, too embarrassed to continue.

Paul squeezed her hand. "Yes, those are all true. She can also be headstrong, determined, and single-tracked. At times, she is pure emotion and responds out of that, unaware of the impact on those around her."

"She is definitely that. Sometimes I want to shake her, but I can't resist her."

"I think you care a lot about Maggie."

"I do. I love her. I know that sounds strange. We've known each for such a short time. But I can't explain it…I…she…"

"Believe me, I understand. The Carson-Baxters have very persuasive powers. I don't have any regrets." He paused as Derek walked into the room. "Speaking of which, there is a good-looking man."

Derek greeted Susan as if they were close friends. He next kissed Paul. Susan noticed the ease they had around each other and hoped she could reach the same ease with Maggie. She accepted the proffered arm as they adjourned to the restaurant at the top of the hotel.

❖

At nine thirty, the band began to play. Shortly thereafter, Maggie entered, microphone in hand as she began to sing. The blue sequined dress she wore highlighted her curves and breasts. Her long dark hair was held back with diamond hair clips that caught the lights and cast small rainbows as decorations in her hair. Diamond pendant earrings and sapphires and diamonds framed her head and wrists. She was elegant and sensuous. The crowd responded. Maggie was in her element. She warmed up the crowd with a romantic song. She might have been singing to the crowd, but Susan felt the words in her heart. After finishing her first set, Maggie joined them at the reserved table. People around murmured, but this was too glittery a crowd to ask for autographs. A sexual energy surrounded Maggie whenever she performed, and tonight was no exception. She was animated and attentive. Susan's body ached to be touched. Maggie's perfume filled Susan's senses when she leaned near to whisper a rather sexual offer into Susan's ear. Maggie briefly touched Susan's hand before going back on stage. This light touch was electric, and Susan was filled with anticipation.

After her second set, Maggie again sat down. For the first time, Maggie was more aroused by the presence of Susan than by her own music. Susan had touched a deep place inside her, a place that had been barren and cold for so long. Tonight she sang for Susan. She wanted Susan to know how much she cared.

"You're beautiful." Maggie's words were only loud enough for Susan to hear. "I never tire of looking at you. And I'm having trouble restraining myself. I'm glad I still have another set. Thanks for being here. You are sunshine in my life. I can't wait to show you how warm, and wet, I am. Gotta go."

As they moved closer to midnight, the band stopped and the crowd joined in the countdown. At midnight, Maggie began "Old Lang Syne" and the crowd joined in. This was a memorable evening for Susan. The tears refused to stop. *For the first time, I am truly, deeply in love.*

Maggie sang until one and then they headed for the reserved hotel suite. As the door closed, a pair of hands pulled Susan into a tight embrace. Maggie's lips were warm and searching.

Derek coughed and asked, "My dear, can't you even say hello before attacking this poor woman?"

Maggie's laughter was as warm as her kisses. "Yes, how boorish. Hello, my name is Margaret Carson-Baxter. And may I know your body?" Before Susan could answer, Maggie rained down kisses on Susan's neck and shoulders.

A knock on the door ended Maggie's attentions as her staff and band entered. More people followed. Music came from somewhere near the windows and people began to dance. Maggie disappeared, but Derek and then Paul asked Susan to dance. Finally, a slow song played and Maggie, dressed in tight-fitting jeans, pulled Susan out to the floor.

"I think your name is on my dance card, ma'am." She wrapped Susan in her arms and floated around the room.

Again, Maggie's scent filled her nostrils and Susan felt her pulse race. Everyone else faded as her body responded to the heat and body close to hers.

"Did you know I'm dancing with the most beautiful woman in the room? Probably the most beautiful woman I've ever met." Maggie smiled at Susan's surprised look. "There's just one thing that would add to your beauty." Maggie pulled out a large diamond and emerald necklace. "I think you add to their beauty. I like to see you in beautiful things, but they pale in comparison to you, Susan. You are so beautiful."

Compliments, especially about the way she looked, were very difficult for Susan to handle. "Thank you," Susan said, "but—"

Sensing Susan was about to issue a denial, Maggie put her hand on Susan's lips. "And I honestly don't think you have any idea how stunning you are." Susan moved closer. Maggie pulled their hips close. She was beginning a slow grind. Maggie ran her hands slowly across the front of Susan's evening dress, barely touching the tops of her breasts.

Grabbing Maggie's hands, Susan whispered, "Come on. We're going to bed."

"Mmm. What has gotten into this lovely, reserved woman? Are you suggesting sleep? No, I guess not." Maggie laughed. Maggie said good night to Derek and Paul and asked Maya to move the party to the bar downstairs.

"Your courage amazes me, Susan." Maggie locked the door. "Just now, the way you led me out of the room. There are so many things about you that just blow me away. The way you put Karl in his place. The control you exerted in the meetings we've had." Maggie moved closer. "The aggressiveness you sometimes show in our lovemaking." She ran her hand across Susan's back. "Your organization, your attention to detail."

"Are you still talking about work?"

"I'm still talking about you. Come on." She led Susan over to the couch. "We can sit and talk, if that's what you want."

"Not fair. You're in jeans and I'm in this dress."

"We can remedy that," Maggie said as she helped Susan undress.

They made love, losing track of time until they were both exhausted. Susan was sure she had just completed a marathon. "No more. Stop."

"But, darling, that's only round one."

Susan groaned and pulled Maggie close, wrapping herself around her. Susan slid her thigh against Maggie's wet center and started a steady pressure and rhythm.

"I love you, Margaret Carson-Baxter," Susan said when Maggie cried out, resplendent in orgasm.

Susan watched her fall asleep and wondered why Maggie still had not said the three words she needed to hear.

CHAPTER SIXTEEN

Maggie felt wonderful. The last week had been fantastic. Her career was moving. Soon she would leave on tour. Two songs were in the top 40 and moving up the charts. Her picture was the number-one draw at the box office, with great reviews coast to coast. "Not bad for a novice," she said. In her hotel room she checked her schedule for the week. "Fuck," she shouted. She picked up the phone and dialed Karl. "Who the hell scheduled the interview this week?"

"You did. Remember? You told Maya you wanted some Florida interviews, and I got them for you."

"How firm is this?"

"Maggie, nothing is ever firm. If you want to stay in the business, however, you don't screw with the media, even local media. It's really easy to be yesterday's news. And even easier to be forgotten."

"I know. I know. Damn, but I don't have to like it." Maggie wondered how to keep her promise to Susan to have free time. "Fuck! Where the hell is Maya?" She called Maya and passed on the task of calling Susan and changing their plans. She promptly arranged for the rest of her staff to meet in her hotel room at noon and prepare for the two p.m. interview. The television interviewer had been promised an hour.

By one thirty, Maggie was dressed, groomed, and rehearsed.

Her staff, including her agent, generally remained present during the interview, but out of camera and microphone range. They wandered in and out discreetly, but they were never out of voice range. Promptly at one forty-five, an attractive reporter, her camera operator, and two staff carrying lights, backup equipment, and recorders arrived. Twenty-five minutes later, equipment and lighting had been set up and the formal interview began. The reporter, Gina Perry, was clearly ecstatic to be getting the interview with M.J. Carson. The first thirty minutes of the interview they covered ground agreed to before the interview: her new movie, her early music career, her recent musical successes, and finally her current stay in Orlando.

"We just completed our new CD and have been getting ready for our next tour. I'll be doing another movie for the Disney people, but right now, I'm here with my family vacationing."

"Where are your children? I haven't seen them."

"My children are not exposed to the media. I want them to enjoy childhood and not have to fear someone is after them."

"Would you mind them going into entertainment or following in their parents' footsteps?"

"No, if that's what they choose. We want them to get an education first. We both did. We feel that helped us make choices in our careers. I know you have more important questions than what my children are going to do in twenty years." Maggie flashed her most mischievous grin.

"In fact I do. I understand you are negotiating some business deals with some locals. Or is a contract signed?"

Slipping on her star persona, Maggie looked directly at the reporter and answered, "Gina, we have a lot of projects under consideration. If I give too many details prematurely, we wouldn't have much bargaining power. We're discussing a couple of projects involving some local people. As soon as things are finalized, Gina, I'll make sure you are the first to know."

"In the last few weeks, you've been traveling with a local resident. Who is she?"

"I told you I'm not talking about business still in the planning stages. Now, let's talk about my upcoming tour." She again smiled, trying to dissuade her questioner from further personal questions.

"I'm not sure this is business. Is it?"

"Excuse me?" Maggie asked.

"There've been rumors of some type of personal involvement. That you and she—" Perry was cut off by Maya interrupting with a phone call.

"I'm sorry, Ms. Perry. I was told it was urgent." Maya handed her the cell phone. Turning to the reporter, she said, "It should take just a moment. Can I get you and your crew something to eat or drink?"

Maggie walked into her bedroom with the cell phone. Karl was on the line. "Where the hell are you? I thought you were still here."

"I am," he answered. "I'm calling from one of your bathrooms. I keyed your number into the phone just in case. Maya and I worked it out."

Maggie laughed and made a mental note to give them a hefty bonus. "Okay, what do I do now?"

"Remain calm. You're playing into Perry's game. Get back in there, apologize for the delay. In ten minutes, get up, shake everybody's hand, smile, be pleasant, then leave with Maya. She'll have you out of here before Perry has time to push the down button. Okay?"

"Thanks. Now I know why you work for me."

"Don't kid yourself."

Following Karl's instructions, Maggie went back in and apologized for the delay, using business as the excuse. "Now, where were we?"

Gina Perry was ready. "Ms. Carson, there's been some mention that this woman may not be involved in a business relationship with you. Maybe something more personal?"

"Ms. Perry, during the last few weeks, I've been spending

time with my family and a few friends. My husband and I have many friends. They remain our friends because I respect their privacy. Outside of the time with my family, I've been dealing with business." Looking at her watch, she stood. "I'm sorry, but I really need to run. My agent will answer any remaining questions. Thank you for coming." She spoke briefly to each member of the news crew. She ended with Gina Perry and thanked her for being understanding. Maya led Maggie to the private elevator and the waiting limo.

❖

Maggie knew she should've taken the rental car but wanted to get as far from the hotel as possible…and quickly. When the chauffeur dropped her off at Susan's house, she noticed some neighbors standing outside their houses staring. "Fuck," she muttered, "there goes the neighborhood."

Children's laughter floated from the far end of the house. She stood and listened. She couldn't remember laughing when she was growing up. Nor could she remember the loud, uncontrolled giggling she heard emanating from her own children. She walked quietly toward the source. In Cady's room, Susan and the children sat on the floor playing a board game. Maggie stopped, mesmerized. Watching Susan, she realized she was experiencing strong, unfamiliar feelings. The closer Susan got, the more frightened Maggie became.

"How's my hugger muggers?" Maggie grabbed D.J. and Beth and wrestled with them on the floor. She saw Cady crawl into Susan's lap while Susan became quiet and tense.

Shit, Maggie thought. *Not tonight.*

Maggie's thoughts were interrupted by Beth pulling out from her arms and asking, "Mom, can we live here? I like playing with Miss Susan and Cady, and we get to see more of you. Could Daddy and Uncle Paul live here, too, and be Cady's daddy? She doesn't have one."

Maggie was lost for an answer. Struggling for a reply, she avoided looking at Susan. "Beth, we have our own house in California. We can visit often…if Susan doesn't mind?" This was a level of discomfort unfamiliar to Maggie.

Susan broke through her thoughts. "Beth, you and your family are always welcome." She swallowed hard, then added, "You can come anytime." Susan lifted Cady and walked out.

"Mommy, is Miss Susan mad at me?" Beth's young voice was fearful. Burying her face in Maggie's lap, she began to cry.

"Baby, Susan's not upset with you. She's probably just upset because I'm late. It'll be all right." She held her children close to her and rocked them, humming mostly to herself.

Maggie held her children and reassured them. Right now, she needed someone to hold her but feared it was too late.

CHAPTER SEVENTEEN

Settling her kids down was harder than Maggie imagined. Once they were calm, she went in search of Susan. Susan was a different kind of problem, one she wasn't sure how to handle. Maggie doubted she was capable of making a commitment. *Nothing is forever*, she reminded herself. The thought of losing Susan was overwhelming. Her hands clammy, she felt the sweat forming, even in the air-conditioned house. "I don't need her," Maggie muttered. Maggie halted her thoughts. She did need Susan.

Maggie wandered into the backyard and found Susan sitting on a lawn chair. The smell of oranges filled the night air. She knelt and reached for Susan's hand and tried to talk, but found speech difficult.

"Look, Maggie…" Susan began, avoiding eye contact.

Maggie put her hand up. "Listen, please!" This was difficult and unchartered territory, and Maggie was afraid. Afraid of her feelings…of losing Susan…of her own ghosts. "Beth didn't know—"

"Maggie, this is not about Beth. This is about you and me. My whole life—and my family's—has been uprooted and we're expected to come and go. Or wait, as the case may be." Susan paused to hold back the tears close to taking control. "I don't live like that. Even my mom doesn't live like that. And I certainly try to provide more stability for my child."

"Susan, please, wait—"

"No, Maggie, you wait. When Cady and I went to my room, she was crying because she thought you and the kids were leaving and she would not see any of you again. She's accustomed to people being around for birthdays, holidays, and for whatever. She loves you, Maggie, and D.J., and Beth. You've become part of our family." She hesitated before looking at Maggie. "And I love you. I have from almost the first moment I saw you. I never knew I could feel such passion, such love…till you." She stopped, wiping tears before continuing. "The really sad part is that I've been afraid to tell you how much because you might run away."

"Susan, you know how much I care about you and Cady." It was true, she did care. Lots of people had told her they loved her. Some said anything for money or a fuck. Love was a matter of convenience rather than an emotion. "I'm here. What more do you want?"

"How about saying 'I love you, Susan. I want to spend my life with you, Susan. I don't want to spend my life without you, Susan.' That would be a good start."

Maggie walked back and forth. The rips in her heart were becoming huge holes. "Susan, you must know how important you are. I don't ever remember feeling this way. I'm not sure I know what love is. Sometimes, when I was little, I would sneak out of bed at night and see my mother sitting at the kitchen table crying. Once I came in and asked what was wrong. She just said, 'No one told me love would hurt like this.' We never said 'I love you' in my house. I made escaping my life until I met Derek. He's my friend. He's always there for me. I love him and I love my kids. That's a different kind of love, one that feels safer, more secure. When Paul came along, I was so afraid of losing Derek that I again focused on my career. In my life, the people who said they love me have left me or used me. Love means pain. Love means leaving. You've changed everything. And now…" She reached over and grabbed Susan's hand. "I want you to be a part of my life. I don't want to lose you, Susan. I don't understand why you love me, or why you stay. I fear you will just go away or find someone else. This damn reporter today was asking questions about you and I can't—"

"What reporter?" Susan pulled her knees up against her chest and wrapped her arms around them as if this simple act could ward off further intrusions into her life.

"Gina Perry, from one of the local stations."

"Perry has a reputation for being a bulldog. What happened?" Susan vaguely recalled Ed's comments about a reporter seeking information and wondered if this was the same person.

"Nothing. She was fishing." The look on Susan's face indicated she didn't quite buy the story. "Susan, please. I don't want to talk about Gina Perry." Putting her head in her hands, Maggie tried to explain. "Meeting Derek in college was a fluke. He became my friend, my first real and only friend, until I became successful. Suddenly everybody was my fucking friend and everybody loved me." She sighed, feeling old and tired.

She took Susan's hand and stroked the palm as she continued. "People tell me they love me all the time. Most of my lovers have said it so easily, and certainly in the thralls of orgasm it seemed to be a requisite. I was more a trophy. Or the friendly banker with deep pockets. Screw the bitch and she'll give you something expensive." Her words were harsh and cruel, born from years of using and being used. "I can tell you I love you if that's what you want to hear. But it's just words. God, if ever there was a time I wanted to be sure about love, it is now and it is you." A sob slipped out, punctuating the moment.

Further comment was halted with the arrival of a car in the driveway. Susan's mother appeared agitated as she parked. Susan stood up, wiped her tears and went over to her mother. "Mom, what's the matter?"

Maureen's Irish temper was in full bloom. "There are

people standing in front of the house, blocking the driveway. Not neighbors. I know everyone in this block. One of them had a camera. I had to threaten to run some people down before I could get in my own damn driveway."

"Who are they, Mom?"

"I don't know, but I'm going to call the police."

Maggie jumped into the discussion. "Why don't we find out what they want?"

Her mother turned and looked at Maggie. "They want to know who drove up in the limousine. And if M.J. Carson is staying here. Apparently you're on the evening news. I told them there is no M.J. Carson in the house, only my family."

"Maureen, I'm sorry. I didn't mean for any of this to happen. The kids and I will move back to the hotel right away."

"You will not. You are a part of this family and I won't…" Maureen hesitated. "It looks like I'm interrupting something. You two talk, I'll go in and check the kids."

"Nothing is going right today. I'm so sorry, Susan." Maggie walked back to the house, unsure of what else to say.

"Mags, wait, please don't leave." Maggie stopped but didn't turn around. Susan walked up and put her arms around her. "Please stay." Maggie nodded but pulled away and went into the house. An icy distance was growing between them that Susan felt incapable of stopping.

Susan listened to the leaves rustling on the orange trees. Most of her life, she had played in this large backyard with its graceful fruit trees and the one large magnolia tree planted many years ago. This had been her refuge. Somehow, it didn't seem safe anymore.

Susan walked into the kitchen. Her mother was with Cady making cookies. Maureen smiled. "Maggie took her children back to their room. I don't know what's going on, but she looks worried, honey."

"I know. What can I do to help?"

"Why don't you get Maggie and the kids ready for dinner? If you want to talk, I do listen."

"Thanks, Mom."

Maggie, D.J., and Beth were sitting on the floor next to the bunk beds. The children were wrapped around her. Susan stood near the door trying to decide what to say.

"Mom, I wanna go home. I miss Daddy and Uncle Paul." D.J. was restless.

"I know. We'll be going home soon. I miss them, too, but I would also miss Susan and her family."

"I wanna go home!"

"Don't you like Susan and Cady?"

D.J. put his head down. Susan's heart was breaking. She sat in front of them. "D.J., I love you and Beth and I love your mom too." Beth's eyes were open but wary. "You two are lucky to have each other. If you go away, we'll miss you."

"You mad at my mommy?" D.J. asked.

"No, D.J., I'm not mad at your mom." Susan spoke to D.J., but looked at Maggie. "I love your mom very much. I want us all to be a family."

"Are you gonna marry my daddy too?"

This drew a smile as Maggie ruffled D.J.'s hair. "No!" She laughed. "Then we'll be in trouble."

"Come on." Susan grabbed D.J.'s hand. "Let's eat. Or my mama will be mad at us."

"I like Gran'ma Mameen," D.J. said. The tension was broken.

As the children ran out of the room, Susan reached for Maggie's hand to help her up. Halfway up, Maggie pulled Susan on top of her on the bottom bunk and whispered, "Thank you. I am trying, Susan. I really am."

So many unanswered questions about her relationship with Maggie still plagued Susan. She lifted herself up and pushed away the questioning. "I know. Let's go eat."

Putting their children to bed was not an easy task. The children were operating at high speed. Susan and Maggie stayed with them until they finally fell asleep. Finally alone in the bedroom, Maggie said, "Thank you for this evening. I wish I could be everything you want."

That night they made love with such intensity Susan couldn't hold back the tears. There was a vulnerability in Maggie, an eagerness and neediness. Susan could not get enough of her. Maggie played her body with such expertise that Susan responded to her touch, her desire, her need. "I love you," Susan whispered as she came. Momentarily she floated between a world of passion and tenderness. The heat rising from Maggie's body spurred Susan and she wanted her mouth on Maggie's wetness and to feel her tremble. They began the familiar dance. Maggie slid up and down against Susan. Before she could taste her, Susan felt Maggie's orgasm.

Maggie wrapped her arms around Susan, fearful of letting go. She needed to feel Susan's body as much as she needed Susan. It was then she whispered, "I do love you, Susan, but I'm scared."

Susan had trouble swallowing. Maggie had finally said, "I love you." Now it was Susan's turn to be frightened. *Will you still say it in the morning?*

❖

Morning came too soon. Susan replayed the evening but again her heart and mind argued.

You really haven't known her that long. What about taking time to get to know her?

Oh, but I know I love her. There is such a thing as love at first sight.

She told me she loved me.

Yes, in the heat of passion. What about the next morning when you're sitting at the breakfast table with curlers in your hair and cream on your face? Think she will repeat that?

I don't wear curlers or cream.

You're avoiding the question. Will she repeat it?

And then it started again.

She curled against Maggie's back and inhaled the wonderful smells of Maggie and sex. Maggie moved against her and purred.

As Maggie turned to face her, Susan asked, "Maggie, do you love me?"

"God, Susan, you know how I feel about you. We have so little time." Maggie began to caress Susan.

Susan sat up and pulled the sheet around her. "Maggie, please, I need to talk. Do you remember what you said last night?"

"What time? Which one?" Maggie sat up. "Hmm, did I say something wrong? Let's see. I promised to fix breakfast."

"I'm serious. Did you mean it when you said you love me?"

"Of course. I always say what I mean."

"Why can't you say it now? I'm beginning to feel this is more about sex."

Maggie climbed out of bed and wandered around the room picking up and inspecting things. "This isn't about sex. I can't imagine life without you and it scares the shit out of me. There are people who use words all the time and don't have what we have."

Susan tried to understand. She wanted to trust Maggie but she also wanted a clearer commitment. At the same time, there were traitors inside reminding her to take one day at a time.

"You touch me in a way I've never known. These emotions, these feelings are all so new. Most of the time I don't understand. And most of my life I haven't tried to." She grabbed Susan's hand. "I've got to go to L.A. for a few days the end of the week. Let's talk when I get back. I need time to try to sort this out."

Susan nodded. "I don't want to lose you. I'm trying to understand. Sometimes I find myself trying to play mind reader. Please don't shut me out."

"I've shared more with you than I have with anyone, including Derek. It's just not something I spend a lot of time doing. I am trying."

"Yes, you are trying." Susan laughed. "I love you. I haven't said that to anyone else outside my family and meant it the way I do with you. I want to know more about you. I want to share my life with you. If you don't feel the same way, I'd rather know now."

Maggie put her arms around her. "There isn't anyone I'd rather be with or rather share my life with. Please be patient."

Susan agreed, unsure of what other recourse her heart had.

Chapter Eighteen

When Susan and Maggie sat down for breakfast, Maureen informed them their neighbor had taken on some people outside of the house. "Genevieve takes our Neighborhood Watch program very seriously," Maureen said. "At first she was disappointed because some of the onlookers were just curious about the limo that arrived yesterday." Maggie choked on her cereal but Maureen didn't notice. "One stranger said he was an investigator reporter. So Genevieve asked him why he was here. He said he'd gotten a call there might be someone important staying in the area. So, you know Genny, she took him inside her house and showed him the family portrait hanging in her living room and offered to give an exclusive interview."

"What family portrait is hanging in her house?" Maggie asked.

"Why, Queen Elizabeth of England and Prince Phillip, of course. Genny is a distant cousin of the prince. She's English and married to an American. I got the feeling the investigator left the neighborhood shortly after their chat." Maureen picked up her empty coffee cup and left.

Maggie looked at Susan and wondered what would happen next.

❖

The day was beautiful and everyone agreed it was too nice to be inside. Maggie called and hastily arranged a trip to Universal Studios. They enjoyed the park and each other for the first hour until Maggie was recognized by one of the local TV talk show hosts. Universal had invited a large number of entertainers from TV and film as part of a program they were shooting for the week. Maggie looked at Susan. "Just give me a few moments. I'm sorry. I didn't know."

Susan shook her head. "Can't take you anywhere. Go. We'll walk on, but hurry. I'll miss you." As she walked away, she watched an amazing transformation as Maggie became M.J. She briefly wondered how Maggie handled it. Sunglasses in place, M.J. greeted the group.

For the next two hours Maggie was frequently accosted and dragged into conversations. Susan tried to be understanding, but each interruption tore away at her reserve. When Maggie next returned to them, she was accompanied by three Universal employees.

"What's going on?" Susan asked.

"The studio is having some kind of party here today. Universal has offered to make sure we'll not have someone following us or interrupting us the rest of the day. I really do want to spend the day with you."

Susan was hesitant but soon realized Maggie's decision was a good one. The Universal escorts enabled them to get on rides and continue the day undisturbed. At the exit gate, however, Gina Perry and her camera operator were waiting for them. The Universal escorts managed to derail them long enough for them to safely leave.

By the time they arrived home, more people and a camera truck were standing around. Susan locked the car doors and pulled into the driveway, in spite of someone banging on the car. Maggie swore. The kids cried. Susan was furious.

"Susan, Maureen, I'm sorry," Maggie said. "I'll get someone out here first thing in the morning."

Susan pushed the remote control and hoped the garage door closed before anyone slipped in. She walked into the house without responding. Only after the kids were in bed did the adults sit down.

"I said I'm sorry," Maggie said defensively.

"I heard you the first time. I'm not angry at you. I just feel violated. Here in my own house."

"Those people are just rude," her mother said. "Maggie is not responsible for someone else stalking her, wanting an autograph or photo, or for someone determined to intrude just to further his or her career." Susan was always amazed at her mother's ability to understand what was going on. "Maggie, I know this is the world you live in. This is not Susan's world. Bless her, she is a bright, talented accountant, but the only autographs she's asked for are on payroll checks. As long as she signs them, the people don't care what she looks like, how old she is, how many heads she has, or whether or not she has teeth.

"Maggie didn't plan this. I've learned she really tries to keep her personal life out of the public's view, especially where her children are concerned. I think you two girls should kiss and make up and enjoy the evening. I'm going to bed. You should too."

Susan wasn't sure how to respond. There were some things that just didn't require an answer. This was one of them.

"She's one hell of a lady," Maggie said. "I think she has some good advice. Let's go to bed."

Maggie called Maya first thing the next morning.

"M.J., it's six a.m."

"I know. I need some help. The media is getting out of hand here and I'm concerned about our safety."

"What do you want me to do? The only way you can be safe is to put walls up or move into a gated community."

"I can't build a fence around her house. First, there's no room. Second, she wouldn't let me. I've got to do something. It's not safe."

"How about moving into the hotel? Never mind. She wouldn't be comfortable in a hotel." The two talked until they came up with a plan.

"I'll be in L.A. in a couple of days. Get going. I want this taken care of quickly." Maggie said good-bye and made arrangements to fly to Los Angeles.

The morning she flew to California, Susan drove her to the airport. Again, they were followed. "Honey, I am so sorry."

"I understand but I don't like it. Maybe I'll get some work done while you're gone."

"Will you miss me?"

Susan reached for Maggie's hand and smiled. "Every day. I won't miss the people following us, but I'll desperately miss you."

"I got you something." Maggie pulled a small box from her bag and put it on Susan's lap.

"Mags, stop buying me things." She grabbed the box and quickly unwrapped it. Inside was a pair of earrings that had "FSU" engraved in gold. "Maggie, how thoughtful."

"It's the right school, isn't it?"

"Yes. Thank you." Susan leaned over to kiss her when she noticed a man with a camera walking up. "Shit." She backed out of her spot and drove out of the airport and then back into short-term parking. "I think I lost him."

"You can drop me off and I'll run to the gate."

"No, I want to walk with you."

"Then let's get a move on, girlfriend." They grabbed the garment bag and suitcase and dashed into the terminal. They checked the luggage and then fled to the nearest restroom. "Make sure the kids are okay and safe. They love being able to play with Cady. I'm afraid they have to stay inside most of the time when they're at the hotel."

"Don't worry. Everyone will be okay. I love you. Now, go!" They hugged and Maggie ran for security. Assured the coast was clear, Susan headed out of the main terminal as quickly as she could.

A week later Maggie arrived back in Orlando on a chartered jet, avoiding the media at the airport. Susan was able to pick her up without being stopped. On the evening before Susan's birthday, Maggie arrived with food and wine to begin the celebration.

"Happy birthday. Derek and Paul send best wishes and wanted me to give you these." Maggie handed packages to Susan. "And this one is from my kids. And this one is from me."

Susan opened Maggie's package and found lightbulbs. She burst out laughing. "So, is this to remind me that you are the light of my life?"

The party ended around nine so they could get to bed early. After Susan left, Maya pulled both Maureen and Maggie aside and informed them the plans for the next day were complete. Maggie couldn't hide her smile.

The following morning Susan arose early and headed for the office before anyone was up. She had a stack of work she wanted to finish before she felt free to enjoy her birthday celebration. At work she was inundated with numerous calls and individuals trying to get interviews. Ed dealt with the media, making sure the company name was mentioned often. It at least allowed Susan to get some work finished. Her formerly mundane personal life had become the topic of everyone's conversation. What little she overheard indicated the rumor mill was busy. She alternated with trying to ignore the often not-so-subtle comments and wanting to run away. Work kept her going.

At four, she was preparing to leave when a call from Maya interrupted her. Maya offered to pick her up from the office. Susan protested, then remembered Ed had borrowed her car earlier. She was smart enough to realize something was going on. Hopefully, a birthday surprise.

Instead of heading toward Winter Park, Maya drove north on I-4. Maya drove farther north, turning off the interstate and driving west until she turned into Groveland Estates. Once one of the largest groves in the area, it was developed into a fenced, guarded, and very exclusive neighborhood. The guard welcomed them once he recognized Maya. Susan watched silently, wondering what they were doing in this area. As they drove she looked at the houses, no, mansions, she corrected herself. She definitely felt out of place. At last they turned into a driveway and another set of gates. Maya pointed a remote control and the gates opened. Susan couldn't imagine who lived in this house.

"Well," Maya said, "welcome."

"This is beautiful. Is this yours?"

Maya stumbled. "I…I didn't. This is yours."

At that moment the doors opened with Maggie, her mother, Ed and his wife, and three screaming children rushing out. Maggie eagerly pulled Susan into the house. "Come on." As they walked into the large entranceway, Maggie announced, "We're all going to live here. I bought it." She waved her arms and spun around.

Susan looked around at the expectant faces and waited for the joke. Everyone was smiling. Susan wondered if she had landed in the Twilight Zone. Perhaps Stephen King had rewritten her life? No, everyone looked sane.

Maggie grabbed Susan's hand and led her through the house, describing the amenities and electronic toys. The solarium had both a pool and hot tub. Swimming instructors were already arranged. A large gym would be built to allow them to work out. In addition, there were rooms for a large office for Susan and a studio/office for Maggie. Her mother had a large room, bath, and sitting area, much larger than the cottage behind the house. There were rooms for servants, guests, and staff. The dining room was huge. The entire family could sit around the table and not touch elbows. Not touch at all. There were fireplaces in the family room and several bedrooms. Televisions and stereos were everywhere.

It took a few moments for Susan to erase the slow-moving fog enveloping her brain. "I don't understand."

Maggie grinned. "I bought it for you. For us," she said. "I figured you wanted us to live together. Make some kind of commitment and we can be safe. It took a while, but I had realtors who saw big paychecks and they pushed paper. Amazing what you can do when you have the cash. Now you won't have to worry about people outside your house or worry about Cady. And your mom can have her own area to rule." Pride shone on Maggie's face.

"What about my house?" Susan asked.

"It's still there. I just moved clothes and a few items of furniture. Things your mom said were impòrtant to you. The rest I bought."

Susan was numb. A huge part of her wanted to scream and swear. Never had anyone dared to turn her life upside down the way Maggie had just done. "Thank you." Trying to salvage any sense of normalcy, she added, "I guess it's time for birthday cake."

Maggie was wounded by Susan's lack of enthusiasm but attributed it to her natural reserve. "We even got a cake big enough for all the candles." She grinned mischievously.

❖

As the last of the guests said good night, Maggie and Susan were left standing alone in the foyer. Maggie was pleased with herself and the evening. "I hope this was the best birthday ever." She leaned in to kiss Susan but was pushed back.

"Maggie, buying a house isn't a commitment." Susan put more distance between them by walking to stand near the staircase.

"I don't understand."

"Just because you buy a house doesn't mean you've made a commitment to me or anyone except yourself."

"I don't go out and buy fucking houses just for the hell of it."

"You don't need to swear."

"Why the hell not? Damn it, Susan, I did this for you, for us."

"But you didn't even ask me. I've lived in that house almost all my life. That is the only house Cady has ever known. I like my house."

"The roof needs to be replaced and the central heat doesn't work, and I've even arranged to get those things fixed. None of us are safe from intruders there. There's not enough room for all of us to live. You've complained about all the problems with that house. This one is new, larger, and has more security."

"It's still my house. What gave you the right to do this? Do you think you can just arbitrarily make decisions and we'll willingly follow along? I'm so furious I can spit."

Maggie didn't know what to say. She had spent a fortune to give Susan this house, to surprise her. What more did she want? "That house was not safe for you, your mother, the kids, or me. After what we've been through lately, I thought you'd be thrilled to be able to come and go without that kind of stress. I would worry day and night. I can't live like that, and won't. I want to be safe and I want my family safe. I want you, Maureen, and Cady safe."

"And I expect to be consulted before any decision about my family is made. I want my life back…the way it used to be. My house, my life, my family."

"What about me? What about my life? What about what I want or need?" Maggie ran her hands through her hair, struggling to keep her emotions under control. "By the time I was twelve, I learned you can never go back, no matter how much you may want to. The only way to go back is to not have me in your life. Is that what you want? Is it?" When Susan didn't answer, Maggie headed for the door. "I'm going for a walk. I'll talk to you after you've calmed down." She slammed the door on the way out.

Susan climbed the stairs, wondering where everyone had disappeared to and how to find them. She sat on the top step and decided to wait. "Someone will find me. Sooner or later." She rested her head on her knees and hoped it was sooner.

Maggie walked around the driveway berating herself. She tried hard not to cry, but it was a losing effort. "I don't understand. All my fucking life people have wanted something from me. Whatever they got, they were grateful for. Finally, I find someone I think loves me for me, and she's the most ungrateful…"

She had let her guard down, trusted, and got shot down. *Well, I won't do it again.* A tear slipped from Maggie's eye and rolled freely down her cheek. As if a signal had been given, more joined, and soon Maggie sat on the lawn, sobbing. She cried for the mother who was too tired to love her, for the family she never had growing up, for never being able to doing anything right. But mostly she cried because she was scared and alone.

Maggie remembered she was going on tour soon and needed to stay in the Orlando area until then. If Susan wanted to sell the house when she left, let her. She didn't give a damn. Until then, she liked the house and would stay. Maggie walked back into the house to claim her territory.

"I'm going to bed," Maggie said and then she walked up the stairs. "You're welcome to join me or take any of the rooms adjacent. They're empty. The children are in the east wing and your mother is in the middle. I'm not going to beg." She couldn't remember ever hurting as much as she did now. *Why have I let this woman into my life?*

"Maggie, I'm sorry. I know you're—"

"Forget it."

"Please, let's not be angry with each other."

"What do you want, Susan? No matter what I give, it doesn't seem enough. I've told you I don't believe in forever and saying 'I love you' is cheap. People say it all the time. I've tried to tell you how special and important you are. I've tried to show you how I feel, but that's not enough. You want everything in black and white. Well, life isn't that way. There are more shades of gray and more ways of loving. I don't want to hurt you, and I don't want to be hurt. I'm sorry I'm not good enough."

"That's not true."

Maggie ignored Susan's comment. "I also have a life. Maybe my job isn't nine-to-five, but that doesn't make it less important. I'm willing to bet I've worked a lot harder at being successful than you have. I've been playing clubs since I was sixteen and had several other jobs to support that one. The first time in a long time I find someone I really care about and…and nothing I say or do is good enough. It's your way or no way."

Susan tried to put her arms around Maggie, but was turned away. "Maggie, I'm trying to apologize. I love you. Please."

Maggie was not ready for appeasement. "You're proving my point. How easy it is to say you love me. Yet you can turn around and attack me. That's love? Keep it."

"You're right. I'm sorry. I apologize. I've always had difficulty with change. Once, in high school, my mom moved all the furniture in the living room and I went bonkers. That's no excuse. It's just…this house…I guess I'm not ready for some changes, but I do love you."

Maggie stared at Susan for a long time. It took all her determination to not run into Susan's arms. Her emotions in chaos, she decided not to fight any more.

"I don't want to argue either. Let's just go to bed." Maggie turned and changed into sleepwear. Susan wasn't aware Maggie owned any pajamas. Quietly, she changed and climbed into bed. They barely touched the entire night.

The awkward truce continued for the remainder of the week. Any efforts Susan made were met with cool detachment. She wasn't sure how much longer she could continue.

Maggie found any attempted conversations draining. She was still angry. A week later, she announced she and the kids were leaving. Some problems with the tour had come up and she needed to be in California until the tour started. Her heart in pieces, she was reluctant to leave without some token or peace offering. "You're still welcome to join me on the tour, if you want. If not, I understand."

"I can't. I've got so much to do here. And I want to spend time with Cady."

"Don't explain. No excuses."

"It's not an excuse. We can visit each other."

Maggie stared at Susan and then shook her head. "Yeah, sure." When the limousines pulled into the driveway, she walked out with a large quiet group following. She hugged and said good-bye to Maureen, promised Cady she would see her soon, and then stood in front of Susan. "Take care."

"You too." Susan hugged Maggie but quickly realized it wasn't being returned. "Please don't leave like this."

Maggie kissed her on the cheek and climbed into the waiting vehicle. She put her arms around her children and stared ahead as the car pulled away.

Chapter Nineteen

After Maggie left, a numbness set in. It was easier for Susan to postpone the pain and still function. Work, including hers, required a level of concentration. Maggie had left only one week ago but each moment had turned into an eternity. Susan had wanted order and peace and she got it. But Maggie was gone. The heart that she had so carefully protected was in shreds and incapable of repair. She had her life back, her daily banal existence, but it was empty. And that hurt more than she thought possible.

With the Winter Park house under repair, she had no choice but to remain in the new house—which was already filled with memories of Maggie. Cady kept asking when they would get to visit again. Like so many things in her life now, she had no answer. Surprisingly, her mother enjoyed the new house, sleeping in a different room each night. When questioned, she simply replied, "It keeps me from being bored."

On the weekend they checked on the reconstruction of their Winter Park house. When they climbed back into the car, her mother and Cady both agreed they liked their new house better. Susan stared at her family and wondered why she was the only one holding to cherished memories of the Winter Park house.

❖

Maggie was tired and irritated. She missed Susan and knew she was taking out her anger on everyone around her, but she didn't care. She tried to focus on her meeting with Paul.

Paul shook his head. "We've been down this road before, Maggie. If you aren't happy with my advice, get another lawyer." He walked out of the room.

"Where the hell does Paul think he's going?" Maggie shouted. "I still have business I need to go over. Fuck him. He can be replaced." Maggie slammed her hand on the desk. "Why the hell do I put up with his shit? I can get another lawyer. I have a tour starting soon. The studios will make sure these things get done."

"Paul can be replaced as your lawyer, but he will not be replaced in this house," Derek said. "Or in my life. I don't know what your problem is. You've nagged me about all kinds of petty crap. Paul hasn't been able to do anything right. The way you've treated your staff lately, especially Maya, I am surprised they still work for you. And the kids are afraid of you and your continuous tirades. You don't want to talk about it and you're not ready to listen. Something has to change. Soon!" He started out of the room.

"Derek, wait," Maggie said. "I can't believe you're taking sides. Not you."

"I'm not taking sides. I don't even know enough about what's going on to take sides. I won't let you tear this family apart. I love you and I love Paul. Talk to me, damn it."

Maggie sat and stared at her hands. "I'm sorry. It's not about you, or Paul, or the kids. I should never have gotten involved with her. She's such an ungrateful b—" She couldn't finish her statement. She knew that wasn't true. "Why couldn't she just leave things the way they were?"

"How were they?"

"You know, things were easy between us. We enjoyed being with each other. We went places together. I loved the time we spent together. She's warm, funny. She has this dimple in her chin that looks so damn cute when she smiles. She's intelligent and…" Maggie paused and then smiled at Derek. "She's one hell of a businessperson. You should have seen her with Karl. God, she's wonderful."

"How did things change?"

"Things got really out of control. She didn't want to go places with me or be with me. She kept wanting to put labels on everything. If things weren't going the way she wanted, something was wrong. I told her I was giving all I could. She kept wanting more. She was never happy with me or what I did."

"Well, that was general enough."

Maggie glared at Derek.

"Come on, Mags, you need to tell me more."

"Instead of spending time with me or traveling with me, she wanted to spend time with her family. She yelled at me because I bought the damn house to keep her safe from nosy people. And she yelled at me because there were too many nosy people around her old house. No way could I win."

"Do you love her?"

"Christ, now you sound like Susan. She thinks that all it takes is to say some magic words and everything is okay. Well, I'm here to tell you it doesn't work that way. I could go out and buy half a dozen people that would swear they were madly in love with me."

"Do you love her? If you don't love her, you ought to move on. Let her go."

"I can't." Maggie's hands shook. She'd gotten along fine before Susan, but she didn't even want to imagine what her life would be like without Susan. She felt more vulnerable than she ever had in her life, and alone. "What am I going to do?"

"I've never seen you happier than in the short time since you've met Susan. You laugh more, seem more relaxed, and seem genuinely happy. And when she looks at you, it's so obvious she adores you. You know, there's nothing wrong with telling her you love her. You tell me and the kids all the time."

"You're my best friend, and you know how much I love you and the kids. This is different."

"Maybe Susan wants to know if you're in this for the long haul. What future do you envision with her? Or do you? Paul and I often talk about tomorrows, whether next week, next year, or ten years. We get excited thinking about growing old with each other. Susan's not a groupie. Talk to her."

"I think I'm falling for Susan."

"Then tell her and give the rest of us some peace. Maybe things are a little rough right now. People like Susan are not throwaways. Is Susan just about sex?" Maggie didn't answer. It was the same question Susan had asked. Derek walked out of the room.

She desperately missed Susan. Maggie could almost smell Susan's perfume. If she closed her eyes, she could feel Susan's presence, actually hear her moving in the room. When she opened her eyes, she was aware of a hollow ache so large it threatened to swallow her. The walls were closing in around her. She couldn't change her life. Keep it light. Never look back.

❖

Maya needed to finish work on Maggie's CD and made a quick trip to Orlando. Susan met her at the airport. "Welcome back to Orlando. I hope your trip went well." Susan walked back through the terminal with Maya. "Do you have any luggage to pick up?"

Holding up her carry-on, Maya smiled. "Nope. Traveling light. I'll only be here for two days, just need to review the contracts and then make sure the recordings are done."

Susan changed the topic to business. "Ed will meet us at the house and we'll review the contracts. This evening we'll have dinner with two of the major players in this venture. There will be—"

"Hold on. Can I wait until we sit down and I can write this down? I'm still trying to adjust to East Coast time."

They agreed to hold business talk until they got to Susan's house. As they were pulling into the drive, Susan realized Maggie hadn't been mentioned once. A part of her wanted to ask, while the other part feared any answer.

The day went smoothly and at five p.m. Ed placed a conference call to Maggie and Paul to discuss the results of the day's work. Maggie's voice floated over the speaker and Susan could feel every syllable resonate through her body. Breathing was difficult as she struggled to remain focused. At the end of the conversation, Susan had to provide some details and did so in as impersonal manner as possible.

Finally, they wrapped up the meeting when Paul said everything was in agreement. "Ms. Carson would like to sign the final contracts as soon as possible. She was wondering if we could have everything ready by the twenty-fourth. We could all meet in your office in Orlando."

"Not a problem." Ed rubbed his hands in excitement. "We'll make sure everything is ready and will have the drafts to you next week." He looked at Susan for confirmation. She nodded, unsure of what else to say.

At the end of the conference call, Susan offered to take Maya to dinner before giving her a ride back to her hotel.

"It was kind of strange tonight. Being out to eat and not having people interrupting," Susan said.

"It's not easy," Maya said, "being part of an entourage. You'll be surprised at the offers I get if I can provide access to M.J. I have had men and women offer money, drugs, Lakers tickets, even their bodies, for a chance to be part of M.J.'s crowd. It can be really tough on the ego to realize you are being offered all this, not for who you are or what you look like, but who you know."

"Maya, I'm sorry. I didn't realize."

"We used to laugh about them at first. But then most of the staff realized that was part of the job. Not pretty."

"No," Susan said, "not pretty."

CHAPTER TWENTY

After the Pro Bowl was over, Derek told Maggie he was retiring from professional football. Maggie, half listening, thumbed through a trade magazine, as he talked about his choices for the future. Her own life no longer seemed safe, or secure.

"Maggie," he continued, "Paul and I are thinking of taking some time off with the kids and going on a cruise for a few days. After we get back, I'm going to San Diego to talk to my parents."

"What's up?"

"I don't want them to be surprised or have to react in case they have to deal publicly with my being gay. Now that the NFL is over, I don't have to lie anymore."

Panic flooded Maggie's every nerve fiber until she was drowning in fear. "Why now? What difference does it make?"

"This lying and side-stepping rumors has put a lot of stress on my relationship with Paul, with you, and even on your relationship with Susan. Paul has been patient, but I'm not taking any chances. I love him, Maggie, and I don't want to lose him."

Maggie stared, speechless. She desperately missed Susan, but she didn't know how to reach across the chasm between them. Once again loneliness enveloped her. "I guess it's fine," she mumbled. "I didn't know you were going...I kind of thought..."

"Thought what?"

"Since your parents have such strong feelings about you being gay, why would you care about telling them? They've never supported you or your lifestyle when you first came out to them."

"My parents may not approve, but I still want to tell them again. They may not be the best parents but they're the only ones I have."

"Do you really want to come out publicly?"

Derek hesitated. "I've been asking myself the same question. I don't know if I'll come out with some big announcement, but I won't lie if asked. How about you?"

Maggie didn't want to think about coming out. She quickly changed the subject. "Hey, maybe we can all fly down to Florida together and spend a couple of days playing before I start my tour."

"How is the tour preparation going?"

"I'm scared." The words flew out before she could edit them. "The concerts I've done are short. Like the AIDS benefits. I don't know if I can do it day after day. Suppose I can't keep up the pace? Suppose I'm not that good anymore? Suppose I—"

"Are you sure you want to do this tour? We have enough money, neither one of us ever has to work again."

"I can't quit now. We've got too many dates booked. What happens if I screw up?"

"The audience won't care. They'll still love you. But if this is really bothering you, why don't you call your agent and have him not book any more dates? We can have time to relax together. You know—like a family."

Maggie laughed. "So traditional. That's one of the things I love about you. You still haven't answered my question about us doing something before I leave on tour."

The enjoyment of planning a family outing was cut short when Derek mentioned having Susan join them.

"Why?" Maggie asked. "Can't we just make it our family?"

"I thought you would want to see her. Besides, whether you like it or not, Susan is part of our family. If we go back to Florida, the kids will want to see Susan and Cady. They've been asking all week when Cady is coming to visit."

"Forget it. It's a stupid idea." Maggie turned and began to climb the stairs to her room.

"Why not?"

Maggie was silent. The possibility that Susan might not want to see her had been avoided. The hole inside her was becoming a bottomless chasm. "Do you think Susan loves me?"

"Susan loves you. You, however, tend to be a steamroller. Susan could be feeling hurt."

"Hurt? What about me? I was only trying to give her what she wanted. It was a safe place to live."

"Maybe she had a different idea about living together and safety. Maybe she has a different feeling about gratitude."

"I don't want her damn gratitude." Sighing, she asked, "Do you really think she still cares?"

"You need to ask her, not me. Whatever you two decide, it's unfair to the kids for them not to spend time together. What I know about Susan, I don't think she turns her feelings off that easily."

Susan stood in the lounge of Executive Airport, questioning her sanity. She was meeting Maggie, Derek and the kids. "I don't know why I allowed myself to be talked into this. They could have rented a car. We could have met in a more public place. Where, Ms. Know-it-all? The zoo? That would be a good place. We could be the exhibit." When she stopped her pacing she noticed people staring at her. *Great, they probably think I'm crazy and dangerous. Talking to myself.*

She glanced out a window and watched a sleek twin-engine Learjet gracefully land. She wanted to run, but the only part of her that was moving was her stomach—up and down, up and down. *It's an ordinary plane. Yes, but there is nothing ordinary about one of its passengers.*

The private jet taxied to the gate. Susan held her breath as the door opened and the passengers deplaned. *I can do this. I can do this.* One part of Susan recognized that she was madly in love with this Maggie. Another part wanted to strangle this self-centered, overbearing ego.

Derek opened the door as the ground crew ran over to assist. Once the plane was secured, he stepped out of the open door with D.J. and Beth pulling on his hands. Next Maggie appeared. She hesitated just briefly, looking around before descending the stairs. Susan's throat was dry and her heart raced. Even at this distance, Susan felt the heat building in her body. She couldn't hide the incredible hold Maggie had on her heart and her body. Susan saw no one else until the group disappeared into the gate entrance. She took a deep breath, closed her eyes, and whispered, "Maggie's here."

A large group entered the terminal, but all Susan saw was Maggie. She was breathtaking, dressed in jeans, a blue broadcloth button-down shirt, and gray blazer. This was the woman she had first met. Susan didn't miss the fact that Maggie looked thinner and tired. At that moment, Susan wanted to be in her arms, the two of them holding each other and talking.

"Thank you for meeting us," Paul said as he hugged Susan and Cady. This was soon followed with hugs from Derek and the children. Only Maggie hung back, not moving or speaking. Susan's heart was in free fall. *She must still be angry.*

Automatic pilot kicked in. "I've made arrangements for a rental car. They just need to see a driver's license."

"Great," Derek said. "Why don't you, Maggie, and the kids head out to the house and Paul and I will take care of the rental car? We'll take the luggage with us." Susan nodded. Once they were in the car, she realized how much more painful it was to have Maggie sitting next to her but not talking. Susan's heart was breaking.

❖

Maggie stared out the window, regretting the trip. From the moment she saw Susan in the terminal, she knew she'd made a mistake. The look on her face was all she needed to know that Susan didn't care. *It's only three days, and then I'll be on tour.* Hurt and rejection dropped in her lap. These were familiar enemies. She fought hard for some semblance of control.

"How's your mom?" Maggie asked.

"Fine. She's anxious to see you."

"I've missed her."

"She's missed you. We...we all have."

Maggie looked to see if Susan was including herself in the "we." "I...I've missed you too. So have the kids." Both defenses were still intact, but a crack was found. By the time they arrived home, light was slipping in the crack.

Maureen warmly greeted Maggie and the children and directed them into the house. Sounding like a general organizing her troops and their movements, she gave orders and directions, telling them to hurry or they would miss lunch.

The day passed quickly with much chattering and laughter. Even Susan and Maggie got into a playful mood. It wasn't until bedtime that everyone realized General Maureen had also carefully orchestrated sleeping arrangements. When Maggie asked about the location of her luggage, Maureen replied, "Why, I put it up in your and Susan's room. You two run up and get to bed. We have a long day tomorrow. You both have work in the morning and then we have plans for the rest of the day."

Maureen, Paul, and Derek made their exit, claiming to be tired. Maggie and Susan were left standing at the bottom of the stairs.

Hesitantly, Susan spoke. "I didn't…I mean, I can sleep downstairs."

Maggie fumbled for a reply. For the last three hours, she had thought of Susan and what it would be like to be lying next to her, talking and holding her. To really hold her. This was not a step in that direction. "No, that's not fair. This is your house. I'll sleep down here."

"No, this is your house too. It was your money that bought it."

"There are enough bedrooms we don't have to fight over which one to sleep in. This is our house. I wanted someplace we could both live safely. Am I that bad a person that we can't share the same bedroom, much less the same house?"

"No, Maggie, you're a good person. I'm sorry. I know you were trying to be helpful. I overreacted. I don't deal well with change, but I'm getting used to it. Well, I'm trying to get used to it."

Maggie smiled at that comment. "I owe you an apology too. There was no reason for me being such an asshole. I wouldn't even listen to you."

"But I wasn't even giving you the chance. I—"

Maggie held up her hand. "Are we arguing over who should apologize?"

Susan smiled and Maggie felt the warmth crawling into her aching heart. "I hope not. That's bad."

Susan put out her hand, "Can we go upstairs and talk? I would really prefer sitting down. I'm tired."

Maggie just nodded and walked quietly up the stairs. Letting time, and sharing, heal some of the distance, they talked and held hands. "I've thought about you every day."

"Me too," Susan said. "I try to imagine what you are doing. We get the press info about your tour at the office. Ed, of course, is in heaven with all the new business coming in." She paused and stared, trying to memorize every feature. "You are so attractive."

"Thank you." For the first time in her life, Maggie believed it. She yawned and pulled Susan closer. When Susan put her head on Maggie's shoulder, Maggie felt the tension in her body escape and she allowed sleep to capture her. It was the first moment of peace she had felt in some time.

Early the next morning, Maggie awoke feeling chilled. Pulling the covers over her, she realized she was on top of the blanket and, lying next to her, was Susan. In a brief moment of vulnerability she was aware of the depth of her feeling, but she was unsure what to do about it. She leaned forward and gently kissed Susan.

Susan, more asleep than awake, stirred and put her arms around Maggie and pulled her close. Susan touched her lips to Maggie's and the women were quickly drowning in each other. Susan wanted her and Maggie could feel it. Confused by the intensity of her feelings, Maggie tried to ignore that knowledge, losing herself instead in the experience of the passion. They knew each other so well, drawing on that familiarity to each lead and follow. Few words passed, only sounds of encouragement and completion. At six a.m., they fell back into a sound sleep. At seven thirty, the general arrived at the door and announced breakfast.

"Mmm. I don't think I can move," Maggie whispered, pulling Susan closer.

"I know I don't want to. What time is it anyway?"

"Seven thirty-five. Eastern Time!"

"Why did I tell Ed we'd meet him at ten?" She listened for the returning warning steps of her mother. A knock on the door assured her she would not be going back to sleep that morning.

"We're awake!"

"Just checking. Better hurry if you're going to eat before you leave for work."

Susan pulled Maggie closer. "Let's dine in bed. We can have the contracts brought here and we'll sign them in bed. And then we can have lunch in bed. You are on my menu!"

"We…We…I mean, you want Ed, Paul, and Maya here?"

"I can't have Ed, Paul, and Maya in here. But I do want you."

Touching Susan and kissing her bare shoulder, Maggie was becoming aroused. "No one will come in until we're ready to come out." She tried to work down to a waiting breast only to find it slide away from her as Susan slid out of bed.

"Come on, let's take a shower," Susan said.

Susan felt alive. The water was beginning to turn chilly when they exited the shower, but Susan barely noticed. She was warm from head to toe. It was during these private times that she most appreciated Maggie. The real Maggie, as she was wont to describe her.

By nine, Paul, Maggie, and Susan were headed to the office. Maggie again was the star as she entered the office and greeted the staff by name. Ed led them into the conference room where they reviewed the contracts. By quarter to ten, the new investors were shown in and conversation became intense. At noon Paul said, "I think we have a deal." Lunch and more talk followed. Finally, at three thirty, the meeting ended with all parties agreeing to meet for dinner the following night at the exclusive Harbor Club in Sanford.

As the time for Maggie to leave grew closer, she acknowledged the increasing tension build. "Why won't you come with me?" Maggie asked.

"I have a job. I have a child. I can't just pick up and leave."

"I'm part of your job. You know Ed won't mind. I want us to be together."

"Don't start, Maggie. I can do so much more for you if I'm here. Besides, I'm just getting caught up from the last time you and I traveled. I was so far behind in my work."

"I could get behind you and we could have some fun."

"Sweetheart, this is my job. Besides, I don't want to be a groupie or a rowdy or whatever."

Laughing, Maggie resumed packing. "It's roadie. And you would never be a groupie...or whatever. You are one of the stubbornest, most determined, most beautiful, most wonderful women I have ever known. When you're not around, I sometimes close my eyes and imagine you being in the room. I can actually see you walking across the room with that absentminded look you sometimes get. I watch the way you turn your head when you're really listening—like right now. Sometimes I can even feel you lying next to me and hear your excited breathing when we make love. But being a groupie—not in my wildest dreams."

Susan felt a lump in her throat, realizing Maggie had revealed more about herself and her feelings in a few short minutes than in hours of talking. "I love you, Margaret Carson-Baxter." Susan kissed her palm and then her wrist, feeling the pulse beneath her lips beating rapidly. She was feeling aroused but something much more intense was slowly seeping through her body. *I want you to love me, Maggie. Maybe, if I love you enough, I can help you heal.* As Susan kissed and caressed her, she felt Maggie emotionally drift away. *No! I won't let you go.* Susan pulled Maggie close. "I love you."

The next morning Maggie was distant and quiet. Her leaving felt like more than just a physical leaving. Susan wanted to grab Maggie and beg her to stay, to wake up with her every day, to live together. *This is crazy. It's just a tour.* Susan walked out of the room, wishing this was a work day.

Maggie was immobile, feeling insecure. Dealing with her own emotions, much less someone else's was unfamiliar territory. She resorted to the familiar—she grabbed her bags and headed downstairs. She spent the remaining time with her kids and Maureen, hoping Susan would at least come to say good-bye.

When the guard at the main gate announced the limo, Maggie felt more pain than she could remember. She still didn't understand Susan's unwillingness to travel with her. Susan had become such a part of her life. Maggie wasn't sure how she would cope without her.

As Maggie opened the front door, Susan finally appeared, as if she knew it was time to say good-bye. She waited until everyone else had said their good-byes. "I'm sorry. I got something for you and hid it, then I couldn't find it. I just want you to know I'll miss you." Susan wiped the tears and watched as Maggie opened the dark velvet box. Inside was a white gold ring with both of their birth stones around a diamond. Inside was inscribed: "Deep inside me."

When she read the inside of the ring, Maggie felt her life shifting. "Thank you. This is the nicest…thank you." She hugged Susan and fought back the loneliness threatening to steal away the joy now occupying her heart.

"That's where you will be," Susan whispered into her ear. "Always."

"Me too." Maggie pulled away and walked quickly to the car. She climbed into the limo, refusing to look back. She feared she wouldn't be able to leave.

As the limo drove out of sight, Susan tried to make sense of the emotional turmoil. *Susan, just shut up and learn to accept.*

CHAPTER TWENTY-ONE

Susan's mother often reminded her children when they were little, "Careful of what you ask for, you might get it." Susan was painfully aware of that reminder. She had her mundane job back, her time with her family, and plenty of free time. Time to miss Maggie.

Her work was still demanding, but all too often conversation would float around to a certain singer. Susan found her concentration, or lack thereof, a problem. M.J. Carson was nominated for a Golden Globe for her performance in *Dining Alone*, and then for an Oscar. Business continued to boom and everyone wanted to ask, or talk, about Maggie.

Susan realized she was continuously asking for people to repeat what they were saying. Finally Ed pulled her into his office and commented that she seemed "a little distracted."

"Are you okay?" he asked.

"No, I'm fine, just early Alzheimer's." Susan's glib answer did not deter Ed.

"Are you sure everything is okay?"

"I'm fine, really." As she walked back to her office, she mentally added, "Except for the fact that my heart is dying."

❖

The tour schedule was altered. Some of the concerts scheduled for October were pulled into February to allow Maggie more time to prepare for her new movie. Maggie filled the emptiness in her life with more work, trying not to dwell on how much she missed Susan. Several times a day she started to pick up the phone, but she felt awkward and unsure of herself. She didn't know how to move forward. "Damn, Susan, this could be so much easier if you were here."

Susan wondered if Maggie even thought about her. Maggie had been gone for a month and had only called twice. She had a fleeting thought that she was just a temporary distraction. "No, Maggie does care about me."

Finally, Maggie called. "How about flying out for a long weekend? I can get away for a couple of days."

"I can't right now. I wish you had called a couple of weeks ago. I could have arranged some time off."

"Why can't you do it now? This is the only break I have for the next month." Before Susan answered, Maggie hung up. An hour later, she called back. "What is so fucking important in your life that you can't give up a few days to be with me? I rarely know when I'll have a break when I'm on tour. Surely the things you're working on can be rescheduled for a couple of days. What do you want me to do? Beg?"

"I'm really busy right now. Most of this is your work."

"Fuck you," Maggie spat out and slammed the phone down.

Two weeks later she called again. "Sorry for not calling sooner." Noise in the background made talking difficult. It was her last night in the United States before leaving for Australia and the international part of her tour. "How are things going?"

"Busy as usual. How's the tour going?" Susan recognized the emotional defenses she was putting around herself.

"What can I say? Cleveland was cold and damp. Denver was cold, but dry. Seattle is just cold. Hold on." A knock on her hotel room door interrupted the conversation. "Hey, babe, my breakfast is here."

Susan looked at her watch. It was almost one on the east coast. Ten o'clock Pacific Time.

"I need to run. One more concert then I can go home for a couple of days. Miss you. Love you." The conversation was short and impersonal.

Susan stared at the phone and wondered how they had begun to drift apart. Maggie had said she loved her, but it seemed so impersonal. More a California thing. Susan wanted to call Maggie back but was not sure what to say or how to say it. When flowers arrived the next day, Susan closed the door to her office and cried.

Weeks later, Paul called and invited Susan to join them at the Academy Awards. M.J. Carson was a hot commodity. She won a People's Choice Award for her music. She had received several Grammy nominations. Her name was everywhere. It meant she was even more recognizable. Susan's desire to finally see Maggie had become so strong she was shameless in her eagerness to accept the invitation. She allowed her heart to lead her.

Everything was arranged for her to fly out to California a couple of days early. Time seemed to drag. Her concentration was strained at best as she mentally envisioned the upcoming reunion. She packed and repacked and drove her mother crazy.

"If you ask for the time again," her mother said, "I'll scream. Go get packed. Do something. You've been moping around, irritated, and short tempered since Maggie left. You get upset when you call and she doesn't answer. And you get frustrated when she doesn't call you back right away. Now you're finally getting to see her and you're still moping around."

"Sorry, Mom. I'm just nervous."

She hugged her. "Just go have a good time. Accept what you have and have a good time."

Susan loaded her luggage in the car and headed for the airport.

❖

In Los Angeles, Susan tried to hide her disappointment when she realized that only Derek was there to pick her up. "Maggie won't be in until tonight," he said. "She's been traveling for at least twelve hours and has quite a few more to go."

Susan was unable to hide her disappointment. "Does she know I'm coming?"

"Yes, she suggested I call you, but only two seconds before I was going to. She wants you here."

Later when they returned to the airport to pick up Maggie, they arrived in a limo, courtesy of the studio. This was not the meeting Susan had imagined. Cameras and reporters lined the exit area. People trying to exit the secured area were dazzled at the glaring lights and cameras.

Finally, nearly the last of the passengers to deplane, Maggie was in the terminal. Dressed in designer jeans and a navy blazer, she was as attractive as Susan remembered. Susan saw the light in Maggie's face and her heart jumped. Time stopped and everyone went into slow motion. The noise, the lights, the people. She tried to imagine what she would say and then panic set in.

"A bit overwhelming, isn't it?" Paul grabbed Susan's elbow. "Let's wait in the limo. It may be a while before they get through the crowd."

"I understand how important it is to promote the movie, but why couldn't Maggie have been allowed to leave the plane quietly?"

"There are some studio execs here. They're going to keep Maggie and the movie in the public eye as long as they can."

In the limo, Paul asked, "Susan, are you okay?" Susan looked down at her hands and tried to understand. "I haven't known you long, but I really like you. If something is wrong, I'm a good listener."

"I feel out of place. When Maggie was in Orlando, I felt like I was losing control over my life. My life focused on where Maggie was going, what she was doing, what we were going to do. And now that she isn't around, I feel just as lost."

Paul leaned back and smiled. "She definitely has that ability to disrupt people's lives. You must feel overwhelmed."

"It's more than that. I don't know where I fit into her life."

"Where does she fit into your life? You seem to be very committed to your job. Very few people ever get where you are in the entertainment industry. Not many, especially women, are financial power brokers. And you are good." He hesitated, then continued. "You had a full life before Maggie came into it. Is there room for her in it?"

Words ran around inside Susan's brain like the Keystone Kops. She was unable to answer. By the time she finally formulated a sentence, the door opened and Maggie was there. She sat next to Susan and put her arm around her. "Home, James. I'm tired."

"God, I've missed you," she said to Susan. Her kiss left no doubt of her sincerity.

Susan pulled her close and soon Maggie was asleep. She awoke briefly only to walk into the house and climb into bed. Susan pulled out a nightshirt and put away the new sleepwear she bought for the trip. "We'll have plenty of time," she said.

Maggie woke up confused. She couldn't remember what day it was or what hotel she was in. A familiar scent finally fully roused her from her dream-filled sleep. She recognized her bed. The scent meant Susan was somewhere around. But not in bed. As she looked at the clock, she was amazed it was almost noon. She quickly showered and dressed.

When Maggie got to the sunroom, she found Susan asleep in a large chair. Her long bare legs hung over the arm of the chair and a book rested in her lap. She looked so vulnerable and innocent. Some protective instinct kicked in. Gently caressing the sun-kissed locks, Maggie struggled with the intense emotions she felt. Startled, Susan dropped her book and nearly knocked Maggie over as she stood up.

"I'm sorry. I didn't mean to wake you up."

"I didn't mean to—"

They laughed.

"I've missed you, sweetheart. You looked so wonderful sitting here. I didn't want to wake you. I just needed to touch you. Guess I'm not very good at leaving you alone."

"Good." Hugs led to kisses as they made their way back to Maggie's room. Each time they made love Susan found another barrier lowered and, with it, passion followed. Susan wasn't sure how it could be, she just knew it was. It was dark outside when they finally lay quietly and began to talk.

"I've missed you. Sometimes, at night, in my hotel room, I would be unable to sleep. I would remember what you felt like, smelled like, tasted like. I would try to recall a conversation or an image. And I would replay it over and over. Finally, I would feel as if you were really there. Then I could fall asleep. Reality is so much better." Maggie took her hand and began kissing each finger. "I want to kiss every inch of you. And then I want to do it all over again. I want to create bunches of new memories."

"I figured by now you would have been bored with me. After all, there must be thousands of willing women throwing themselves at you."

"That's true," she answered nonchalantly, kissing the inside of Susan's arm.

"You can be less agreeable."

"I want to be very agreeable. I want to make love with you until neither one of us can walk. We'll have to stay in bed for at least another day."

"I don't think so. Besides, we have to get dressed up and go out to a big dinner tomorrow. So at least one of us needs to be able to walk fairly well tomorrow. Especially if you have to get up and give an acceptance speech."

Maggie groaned. "That would be nice, but the competition is tough. I'm this upstart newcomer. Remember? I'm pleased with all the recognition, but… Maybe one day."

"If you don't think you're going to win, why did you come back?"

"One, my studio insisted. Second, and most important, I wanted to get laid."

Susan sat up and stared, unable to determine if Maggie was kidding.

"Only by a certain someone." Maggie began to crawl toward Susan, forcing her to lie back down on the bed. She leaned over her. "Didn't you think about us in bed, naked, making love? How about my kissing your neck?" She gently nibbled Susan's neck. "Or about my hand sliding up and down your thigh?"

Susan lost her ability to listen to anything Maggie said. She felt the kisses, the caresses, the warmth. Her senses were drenched in Maggie's touches. Susan felt herself letting go of any reserve and joining Maggie in this familiar dance.

❖

"I'm sorry if I'm keeping you from resting." Susan smiled as Maggie choked down a sandwich. "Someone's worked up an appetite." They had gone to the kitchen in search of food after their lovemaking session.

"No, it's okay. I'm just hungry. I mean I enjoyed being with you today. I mean…I mean, being with you is very relaxing, no matter what we're doing. Don't you dare go away."

Putting on her best Southern accent, Susan said, "Why, thank you. You are most gallant for saying such nice things about me."

"Do you suppose you could whisper sweet nothings to me while we make mad, passionate love? That would be so exciting."

No one else was in the kitchen but Susan felt the heat travel up her body. They went back to bed and resumed the lovemaking, this time with a slower tempo.

Susan trailed languid kisses up and down Maggie's body, enjoying the sounds coming from her. As she listened to Maggie's breathing, Susan reveled in the power she enjoyed every time Maggie groaned. She nipped the inside of the well-muscled and tanned thighs. Moving up to the damp crotch, Susan inhaled and enjoyed the scent of arousal. Making love with Maggie was a miraculous experience, far beyond anything she could have wished or hoped for.

Susan looked up Maggie's body, noticing her hand grabbing the sheets. She let her tongue dance in the wetness, Maggie's body arching in anticipation. Susan couldn't get enough of Maggie. She devoured her until she felt the spasms begin. Susan slowly slipped her fingers inside and Maggie rode quickly to orgasm. Susan felt her own control going. As Maggie peaked, Susan's own body responded. Her hand in place, she slid onto Maggie's leg and allowed her own orgasm to fill her. The sheer power of the moment consumed her. She pulled her hand free and felt Maggie pull her tightly against her body. It was then that she felt Maggie's sobs.

"Maggie, oh Maggie, I am sorry." Susan tried to pull away.

"No. Don't move. Please, just listen." Maggie held on tightly. "I'm scared. You were making love to me and suddenly I couldn't control my feelings. It scared me. I wanted you to make love to me. I wanted to feel all those things, yet I wanted to run away at the same time. And then…everything became so intense, I couldn't control what I felt. I love you so much and I'm afraid you won't love me that way. Please just hold me."

The words were flung out, a challenge to Susan to love. Susan remained atop Maggie, struggling for some type of reassurance. By the time she could respond, Susan noticed that Maggie's breathing had changed. Maggie was asleep! Susan vacillated between rejoicing that Maggie loved her and fearing that tomorrow would bring denial. Finally, her mother's words came back to haunt her. *Why can't I accept today and enjoy it?*

CHAPTER TWENTY-TWO

Susan awoke early the next morning and lay in bed next to Maggie, hypersensitive to every move and sound Maggie made. Susan would briefly doze, then awaken when Maggie moved. Only when she was sure Maggie was asleep would she allow herself to relax and doze again.

Finally Maggie was awake. "Good morning, gorgeous. I'm not sure what you did last night, but I slept soundly. You could make a fortune putting lonely lesbians to sleep." Maggie stretched, her naked body resplendent in the morning light. "God, I needed some sleep." She turned and gave Susan a long, warm kiss. "Do you suppose we could arrange a replay sometime soon after this awards thing is over?"

Seeing the questioning look on Susan's face, Maggie quickly added, "This may sound trite, but it's true. I've never experienced whatever happened last night. I don't understand. It felt wonderful and scary. I meant everything I said. I love you."

Tears glimmered in Susan's eyes. She leaned in and kissed Maggie, hoping that the love she felt was being felt in Maggie's heart.

"Give me some time. I'm still trying to figure all this out."

This time Susan eagerly nodded. "Promise." The moment was broken when the phone rang. Breakfast was ready.

❖

The mood changed drastically as they dressed for the evening's events. Members of Maggie's staff were in and out. Susan returned to the bedroom and dressed. She was surprised by a knock on the door. Susan opened it to find Paul in a tuxedo.

"You look stunning. Come on. Let me escort you downstairs before someone else steals you away. Don't want to be late."

Susan worried briefly about Maggie. "Paul, are you really this nice, or does Maggie pay you to take care of her girlfriends?"

His laugh was hearty. "First, I would never work for Maggie. I may represent her legally, but I do not work for her. I would be bald. And you know how vain we gay men are about our looks. Second, you're the only girlfriend Maggie has had in the almost five years I've known her. From what Derek says, you're the only one she has brought home. That makes you very, very special in this household. Third, I do not pimp. Believe it or not, I just want to know you better. You and I live in worlds very different than Maggie and Derek. I hope you'll be my friend."

Such a gracious plea could not be refused. At dinner, she found Paul's conversation and humor almost as enjoyable as Maggie's. Susan looked at her dining companions. "I can't believe this is happening. Maggie, I am so proud of you."

Maggie looked around and then lowered her voice. "I hope you're not talking about my acting."

Susan rolled her eyes. "Yes, I am. I'm not going to ask what you were thinking about. You're an incredibly talented woman."

"Coming from you, that means a lot to me. Now I just need to survive this evening and then I'll show you how much."

"What if you win? Don't you have to party?"

"I don't expect to win. We'll make the rounds to the governor's party and Elton John's. But I just want to spend as much of the time I have here with you. Alone."

"Well, let's get the evening over."

At the awards ceremony the focus shifted to the stage. Even

sitting in the audience, Susan was awed by the well-known names giving and receiving awards. She was thankful for the anonymity of the auditorium. "Ed would be in heaven."

Maggie laughed. "Ed would be passing out cards faster than some of these dancers can tap."

One of the early awards was Best Supporting Actress. Maggie briefly grasped Susan's hand before grabbing Derek's arm. She listened to the names of the nominees, smiling and looking at Derek when her name was called. She was well aware the cameras were on her.

"And the winner is…M.J. Carson for *Dining Alone*."

The win was totally unexpected. Maggie slowly rose from her seat. Derek pulled her into a hug, then pushed her toward the stage. Her costars nearby hugged her and offered congratulations.

The statue in hand, Maggie stumbled for words. "I didn't expect this. I really didn't. I didn't even write an acceptance speech. Oh, I hope my agent doesn't hear that." The audience laughed. "I promised I would." More laughter. "I want to thank so many people." Susan was amazed at how many people Maggie named. "And, most of all I would like to thank my best friend who has always believed in me, even when I didn't, my husband Derek Baxter. This one is for you, Derek." Laughter and applause followed her off the stage.

Derek left to join Maggie backstage. The remainder of the evening was a blur. Cameras and reporters followed them wherever they went. A round of parties followed. Everywhere she went, Maggie was expected to answer questions and be interviewed. An entourage of studio, press, and well-wishers followed. Around two in the morning, Paul and Susan had enough.

"How do you handle this?" Susan asked.

"I love Derek. He's very competitive, a trait essential for success as a football player. With success comes fame, interviews, endorsements, well, you get the idea. I prefer leading a low-profile life. That was rough. The hardest part, though, was dealing with his paranoia about his career. We've really had to work through some very painful times. Through it all, I never stopped loving him. Times like tonight, this is work for them. It may seem like a party to us, but out here, this is work."

"It's hard enough for me to put up with the business lunches and dinners. I don't think I could do this night after night. Maybe I'll just sit home and let Maggie party." Susan yawned. "Can we go? I think I need some sleep."

❖

The next morning was a blur of activity in the house. Maya arrived at seven and Maggie's agent arrived ten minutes later. By eight, the house was full of people and the phone rang incessantly. Ed called twice.

It was nine in the morning by the time Maggie got home. She was still clutching her Oscar and was truly a star. Susan walked around the edge of the crowd and finally wandered into the kitchen. Would it ever be possible to have a long-term relationship with Maggie? The impact of Maggie's winning finally sank in. Susan felt the uncontrollable need to flee back to Florida. To her house in Winter Park. To someplace familiar, safe, comfortable. Quiet.

Maggie wandered over and clutched Susan's hand. "Can you believe it? I even had to do an interview with Katie Couric this morning." Their conversation ended with someone pulling Maggie away. The remainder of the day was even less encouraging. The studio arranged a press conference to announce Maggie's next picture, to be made in Florida, followed by a press party.

Susan looked at her ticket and wondered if she should leave early, but she wanted any time she could steal with Maggie. That evening she almost changed her mind. A reporter from Orlando had tried several times to talk with her, and Susan had barely managed each escape…until she was trapped in the women's restroom.

"Hi, my name is Gina Perry. I believe you came here with M.J. Carson?" Susan tried to head back out the door. "Wait, I just wanted to talk to you. She's quite an attractive woman, isn't she? By the way, you didn't give me your name."

"Excuse me, but I would like to get out the door."

"Look, I just thought that since we were both from Orlando, we would just chat and let all those Californians hug and schmooze. You're the woman in Orlando she's been visiting, aren't you?"

Susan ran into one of the stalls. At that moment, she was more debilitated by an overfull bladder. Hoping Perry would leave, she stayed in the stall. When Susan finally exited, Gina Perry was still there, a grinning Cheshire cat.

"This can be just between us girls, but is she good in bed? I've heard lots of stories."

"Please excuse me." Susan made a more concerted effort to leave, but Perry blocked the door.

"Listen, Carson may think she's a big star, but no one brushes me off. Do you understand? Now, if you help me, I won't mention your name. If you don't cooperate, well, I hope you don't have any secrets." Her smile was vicious.

The standoff ended with the entry of Maya into the restroom. "Oh, there you are. I've been looking for you." Maya took Susan's arm. "You will excuse us, won't you? Say, you look familiar. Have we met?"

"Yes, a few months ago, I met you in Orlando. Gina Perry."

"Of course, with Channel 7 in Orlando. How nice to see you again. Have you had a chance to say hello to M.J.? Please, let me get Susan back to her friends and I'll make sure you get to talk with M.J. Your station probably would like to run an interview." With that, Susan was escorted safely away.

Susan rejoined Maggie and Derek. "Maggie, I think I'm going to go."

Maggie was still enjoying the attention and the limelight.

"Stay. The parties are just starting. When the staff prepped me on these events, they told me the parties go on well into the next day. I still can't believe it."

"Something just happened. Some reporter from Orlando followed me into the restroom."

"Yeah, I know. Maya told me she was going to rescue you."

"Don't you care about Gina Perry and what she's trying to do?"

"Fuck her. Come on, let's get something to drink."

"Maggie, I am trying to talk to you."

"I don't want to talk. I don't care. Forget it. Tonight I just want to celebrate."

"Even if someone wants to destroy you. Why all of a sudden don't you care? You've been telling me how much you protect your private life."

"Look," Maggie said, "I said forget it. Right now I don't care about some stupid reporter." One of the reporters from a national network feed walked up. "Hang around and have a drink. I'll talk to you later." Maggie turned to the reporter and began talking.

"Sorry, she's a little wound up tonight," Derek said. "This has been quite an evening. She feels it's making up for all the years she struggled."

Susan stared at Maggie and then Derek. "I'm tired. Tell Maggie I've gone back to your place." Fifteen minutes later Maya was driving Susan back to Maggie's house.

"I saw Perry go in there when you did. Are you okay?"

"Does shark bait have any meaning?"

"Ouch. Sounds pretty bad."

"She was only interested in my relationship with Maggie. I felt so violated."

"I saw that viper go in. I'm just sorry I didn't get there sooner."

"She seems set on outing Maggie. I can't believe it. The story around Central Florida is that she's closeted herself. How could she do something like that?"

Maya pulled into the drive at Maggie's place. "There are lots of people like her around this place. There are good people too. Just not as many. That's part of my job. Keeping those people at bay." She stopped the car and let Susan get out. "Can I do anything?"

Susan walked around to the driver's side of the car. "Thanks, Maya. No, there's nothing you can do. I don't know how you folks live like this day after day. I've just gotten a taste and it's not something I can honestly say I feel comfortable with. Good night."

Susan changed clothes, putting on lightweight fleece pants and one of her many short-sleeved FSU T-shirts. She sat out by the pool for about an hour trying to read but with no success.

"What the hell am I doing here?"

It was after ten the next morning when Maggie and Derek got back from another round of interviews and parties. Paul was nowhere in sight. "What happened to Paul?" Susan asked.

"He left not long after you did. He's got depositions out of town for the next three days." Derek turned to Maggie. "And I have an interview tomorrow with ESPN. Good night, ladies. Maggie, congratulations one more time."

After Derek was gone, Maggie sat in one of the bar chairs. "God, what a wonderful evening. Would you believe I had people coming up to me and asking me to call them? Some of those fuckers wouldn't even return my calls five years ago. Screw them all." She sat her Oscar on the table.

Susan tried to smile but her encounter with Gina Perry still worried her. "I am proud of you."

Maggie grinned. "Me too. I'm proud of me."

"Maggie, I hate to be a nag, but what about Gina Perry?"

"Oh, God, Susan. I don't want to talk about her now. Can we just drop it?"

"Okay. What do you want to do instead?"

Maggie walked over and pulled Susan into a tight embrace. "I want to fuck your brains out."

Susan could feel arousal starting but the need to talk was stronger this time. She pulled back. "Later? Okay?"

"I am so turned on right now. I'm not sure I can wait. And…I have a photo shoot, an interview, and Karl may be working on a three-picture deal. So you better grab me while you can."

"I thought we were going to spend time together."

"We have. We will. Right now, I'm a hot property and I have to take advantage of this opportunity. Karl also thinks there's interest in shooting some footage of my tour and then selling it to HBO or Showtime." She grinned at Susan. "Don't you want some of me?"

"You know I want you, but right now I would love to have some quiet time and just talk. Like an ordinary couple. Talk about our day, our plans. It seems we haven't had much time together and when we are, we're either in bed or arguing."

"Give me a break." Maggie walked around the room. "Don't you get it? I don't have a nine-to-five job. I can't predict what's going to happen, when I'll have another opportunity like this, or when I'll have down time. I need to make the most of whatever happens."

"Why is it that we rarely talk about us, about our future, about our plans, about our challenges? Except when you want to talk. You make decisions for us and don't even consult me. Then you claim you have to hide our relationship. Why is it you've been telling me that you need to keep your sexual orientation hidden, all of sudden you don't care that Gina Perry is determined to out you?"

"Oh, for God's sake, Susan, why do you always have to mess things up?"

"Me? Mess things up?"

"This is one of the greatest nights, er, days of my life, and you want to talk about Gina Perry. I want to talk about me. Do you know how hard I've worked to get where I am? No one helped me. I worked damn hard and I'm still working hard. Do you have any idea what I go through on tour? Why can't you let me enjoy this?"

"I've told you how proud I am of what you have done, how excited I am for you. What more do you want?" Susan was beginning to get angry. Fatigue and confusion had taken its toll.

"Nothing, Susan. Just leave me alone. I don't need this. I've got a photo shoot and interviews and I don't need to be listening to this. I just want to enjoy my success for once without any heavy conversation." Maggie stomped out of the room. By the time she had showered, dressed, and returned to the kitchen, Susan was gone. Searching through the house was fruitless. Finally she ran outside. Susan was sitting on the steps with her luggage nearby.

"Where are you going?"

"Home, Maggie. Where I belong. I know this is a big time for you and I'm sorry if I ruined it. I don't know what you want from me. I don't understand your life, but I'm trying. I'm not going to just make myself available and then sit around and wait for you to make time for me. And I'm not going to let anyone talk to me the way you just did."

"What a drama queen. I flew here to be with you."

"No, you flew here for the Oscars, and I flew here to be with you." She looked at her watch. "I've been here nearly sixty hours and, excluding sleep and sex, you and I have spent less than ten of those hours together."

Maggie rolled her eyes and wondered how the day had fallen apart. "I'm sorry, but this is my career. And this is my chance to solidify my future, make some money, plan my future."

"What future? Being richer or becoming more famous?"

"Both. What's wrong with that?"

"Nothing, Maggie, except I don't find any room for me." She grabbed her bags and started toward the approaching cab.

"If you leave, it's over," Maggie shouted.

Susan stopped and took a deep breath. "My feelings don't

change that quickly. If you figure out where I fit in your life, you know how to get in touch." Her throat tightened and she struggle to keep from crying. "I still love you."

"Yeah. And you're walking out on me, like everyone else."

❖

Troubled dreams kept Maggie from sleeping. Her anger and comments the previous day haunted her. She had avoided thinking about Susan's leaving by immersing herself in the demands of her latest award. At ten she decided to get up and start preparing for the interviews, then she could devote the rest of the day to the tour. As she was dressing, the phone ring. Sure that it was Susan calling and apologizing, she said, "Hello, and no need to apologize."

"Hello to you, and I don't know what I've done."

"Derek, sorry, I was expecting someone else. I didn't check the caller ID. What's up? How did the interview go?"

"Great. I'm heading to the airport now. What are you and Susan doing tonight?"

"She's not here. She left yesterday."

"I thought she was staying until tomorrow. What happened?"

"I don't know. I wanted us to celebrate and she kept wanting to talk about problems. Can't she give that a rest for a few days?"

"Maggie, do you ever think about how your behavior affects other people? I know we've all been guilty of giving in."

"Giving in. What are you talking about? I'm the one who does the giving in. I give, give, give. Well, I'm tired of it."

"This may surprise you, but there are some people in your life who are not takers. Susan is one."

"She'll change her mind."

"I don't think so."

Deflated, she sat in the nearest chair. "I don't believe it. She'll call."

"Tell me what happened."

Maggie gave an abbreviated version of events. "Maybe I should fly to Orlando."

"And do what? You have interviews and appointments you agreed to. You have no free time left until your plane leaves to rejoin the tour. You really screwed up this time."

"What are you talking about? I can't believe she left. She's just like everyone else." Tears rushed out and a deep dark pit settled in the middle of her chest "I don't cry, and this woman makes me cry! Fuck her."

CHAPTER TWENTY-THREE

Coming back from California, Susan felt death was preferable to the constant pain in her heart. She avoided dealing with her feelings, filling her time with any activity that didn't require serious thought. She tried to move her family back to Winter Park, but reluctantly agreed to a compromise. She was a nomad, traveling back and forth between the two houses. Neither one felt like home, and both held too many memories of Maggie. No place was safe.

Her life returned to a fixed schedule—leaving for work and returning home at the same time every day. She forced herself into an orderly life.

Three weeks later, the phone rang at three in the morning. Groggy, Susan reached for the phone fearing something terrible had happened to her sister and her family. It was Maggie calling from Poland. A rowdy party in the background made conversation difficult.

"Guess what? We sold out in fucking Poland."

"Congratulations." Susan was slowly waking up and wondering why Maggie was calling.

"Next week, I have the whole week. I was on the Internet and found a wonderful villa to rent on Lake Como in northern Italy. We could have a wonderful week there. I can have the ticket at the airport today."

"No, Maggie."

"Why the hell not?"

Susan kept her voice calm. "My boss, my family, and my job need me," she said. "You don't."

"Ow, that hurts."

For one brief instant Susan thought about apologizing, but she had yet to hear an apology from Maggie.

"Listen, Susan, I didn't mean that the way it sounded."

"It's three in the morning. I'm really tired and I need to get some sleep." Susan knew that if she talked much longer she would be pulled back into Maggie's life.

"I'm sorry. I forgot about the time change. I am really serious about you coming over. I...I miss you. Hey, quiet down. I'm sorry, I didn't hear you."

"I've got to go," Susan said and quickly hung up.

❖

"Fuck her," Maggie muttered as she slammed the phone down. "Who the hell is she? Hanging up on me."

"Hey, boss, what's up? Why aren't you partying with us?" Maggie's guitar tech Blair downed another shot of Polish vodka. "This stuff is good. I wonder if we can take a case back."

"Sure. Arrange it." Maggie walked off, looking for a quiet place. Her life was coming unglued. Needing a quiet place, she returned to her room, trying to lock out the loneliness and the fear growing inside her.

❖

Hanging up on Maggie didn't make her go away. Three of her current releases received frequent air play. Susan started listening to classical music. At the office, Maggie was the frequent topic of conversation. Susan hid in her office. Paul called at least once a week. While she enjoyed talking to him, he served as a reminder of Maggie.

By the time Susan was able to get through a day, Maggie again called. Susan was at a meeting and her mother answered. When she got home, her mother nagged her to call Maggie back. Susan postponed calling, hoping the urge, and the need, would go away. It didn't. Reluctantly, she dialed.

Maggie poured herself a drink. God, she wanted Susan. Why didn't she call? Looking around the room, she knew there were a half dozen women in this room she could have sex with. Willing, easy women. No questions asked. Why, then, did she still want Susan?

"Did you say something? Want something, M.J.?" An attractive, short redhead slipped onto her lap, leaving no doubt what she was offering. Maggie wasn't interested. She barely heard the phone ringing over the noise. Blair handed her the phone.

Maggie tried to get rid of the woman on her lap. "Susan, hey, wait a minute." Moving the phone aside, she said, "Cut it out. Leave me alone, damn it." By the time she returned to the phone, Susan had hung up. "Fuck! Fuck! Fuck!"

Stumbling over to the bar, she poured another drink, and then another. She was well into getting drunk when the redhead began to nibble on her neck. Why not? she thought. Pulling the woman close, Maggie began kissing and caressing her.

"Rhonda, my name is Rhonda."

"What?" Maggie muttered.

"My name is Rhonda. You called me Susan."

Angry, Maggie stood, dropping the redhead on the floor. "Get out. All of you, get out!"

"What's the matter, boss?" Alarmed by the shouting, Blair rushed up.

"Get everyone out of here. Now." Maggie slammed the door, leaving the group stunned.

The next day began with a frustrated Maggie finishing off the bottle of bourbon and going back to bed. At two, the phone ringing roused her enough to reach for it. "Susan?"

"Afraid not. Hi, honey. Sorry. Has Susan called? Are you okay? You sound funny."

"Hi, Derek. I'm okay. Long night. I was just getting up. We leave for New York tonight. I'm getting tired of traveling. How are you? How's Paul? The kids?"

"That's part of the reason I'm calling. We thought we'd meet you in New York and spend some time together. How does that sound?"

Maggie tried to focus, but was losing the battle. "What? I'm sorry."

"Maggie, are you okay?"

"I told you I'm tired. I screwed up." She brushed away a tear before continuing, "And Susan hung up on me yesterday. This has been one shitty week."

"I'm sorry. Listen, we'll be at the airport when you arrive in New York. What can I do?"

"I don't know. Why won't she talk to me?" Realizing how tentative her sanity was, she changed the topic long enough to talk to the kids. Later, her head pounding, she packed and headed for the airport.

As Derek, Paul, and the kids greeted Maggie, cameras and microphones recorded every moment. "Who the hell called the press?" Maggie yelled as she crawled into the car.

"Hey, Maggie, calm down," Paul said. "You're scaring the kids."

"Sorry, I'm tired. I told Karl no press. When I find out who did this, I'm going to fire him or her."

"Maybe your tour sponsors are doing this."

"I don't fucking care who."

Derek spoke through clenched teeth. "Your language, please."

Maggie put her head on the back of the seat and went to sleep. She woke up when they arrived at the hotel. "I'm tired. Come on." She took her kids' hands and walked into the hotel lobby, where she was greeted by the day supervisor who personally escorted her to the penthouse elevator.

"Have a good day, Ms. Carson."

When they arrived in the suite, Maggie excused herself long enough to shower and change clothes. When she returned to the living area, she found dinner had arrived. She played with the kids for a few minutes and then went to bed.

The next morning Maggie was cheerful and rested. Tension was thick, but she was determined to ignore it.

"Do you want to talk about Susan?" Derek asked.

"Nope!" Smiling, she changed the topic. "What have you two been up to?"

"Maggie," Derek began hesitantly, "I've been approached to speak at National Coming Out Day in Los Angeles. I said no, but I may want to at some time. I'm not the only gay man in the NFL, but we're all too afraid. Maybe I can help to open the door."

"What about your career?" Maggie's own fears drove her questions more than her concern about Derek's future.

"You know we talked about someday coming out. There is never a perfect time. It's more a matter of our choosing the right time before we're forced to deal with someone else outing us."

The years of hiding were a part of her. She wasn't sure she would know how to not be afraid. Then she remembered the last argument in California with Susan. She had said she didn't care. Which was it? "Have you heard from Susan?"

"We've been talking to Susan at least once a week. We also spent Labor Day weekend with her and her family. She's still in love with you."

"You what? I can't believe this. I thought you were on my side."

"This is not about sides," Paul said. "This is about friendship. She's a friend. Our friend and your friend."

"Friend? She's not my friend. I've made numerous attempts to talk to her, at least six or seven times, and in the last six months she's only called once. Once. I've repeatedly tried to get her to join me for a short vacation—anywhere in the world. She keeps saying no. She's too busy. The first chance I get away from my tour, I invite her to join us. She leaves without even saying good-bye. What do you want me to do? Bow down and kiss her feet?" She paced around the room. "In the last five years, I have been sexually involved with one woman. One! And I was saving myself for this. Fuck that. What else could I have done? I tried to do everything Susan asked. What more could I do?"

"How many times did you tell her you love her?" Derek asked. "How many times did you ask her what she wanted to do? How many times did you call her in the middle of the day and just say you were thinking about her? You and I are so used to having things our way. Paul and Susan are not people you buy."

"How many times did she call me? How many times did she include me in her plans? How many times did I walk out on her? I tried, Derek. But Susan always wanted more." Feeling her emotions drowning her, she stopped. "Enough. I'm going to bed." She stopped, took a deep breath, and then said, "Paul, I'm sorry. You've been a good friend. I don't know what I'd do without the two of you. You are my only friends."

"Believe it or not, Susan is too. She still loves you," Paul said.

"Thanks for the advice," she answered angrily and fled to her bedroom. She leaned against the closed door and cried. "God, Susan, I need you."

CHAPTER TWENTY-FOUR

The rehearsal went badly. Maggie was irritable with the band, the technical crew, with everyone. The hole inside her gnawed and grew.

Performing was raw energy. She had forgotten how it felt. The power. The control.

They had six upcoming concerts scheduled in the South—Nashville, Memphis, New Orleans, Miami, Orlando, and then Atlanta. Maggie was looking forward to returning to Atlanta. It was the Orlando concert she feared the most. Every night she was haunted by memories of Susan.

In New Orleans, she sat up all night after the concert. She put the picture of Susan that she carried everywhere on the bedside table as she wrote. "What a kick. I've written this one for you. I've wanted to say these things to you, but I didn't know how. Now, maybe it's too late." She touched Susan's picture and put it back on the table. Satisfied with her work, she was able to sleep soundly, if only for a few hours, for the first time in months.

The next day was an off-day and then a day of travel. She called her band together midmorning. "I've written some new music. I want to include it in the show. Tell me what you think." The band listened for the next twenty minutes as she went through each song.

"Man, M.J., that's some of the best music you've written.

How do you want to play it?" The drummer was already tapping away at rhythms.

"I thought we could put it in the second half of the show. I want to include it in Miami, but that will mean a lot of practice today if we're going to do it. It would be great because we have a recording session scheduled after Atlanta and we could start out with these. Can we do it? Get it into the show in a couple of days?"

They talked about how hard it would be to work out the music, but the songs were so powerful the band signed on to work all day and during the travel to get the music down. Maggie was thrilled. The band liked the music as much as she did. For the first time in a long time, she felt some measure of peace. But she still wanted and needed Susan to feel whole again.

As with every concert, Maggie donated a large block of tickets to the local Susan G. Komen and AIDS groups as a fundraiser and arranged seating up front. Maggie insisted stairs be placed at the front of the stage so she could come down and meet some of the people. The security people, concerned about her safety, tried to form a buffer around her. She insisted she be allowed to meet the fans. She would walk around and find someone in the audience to sing to. The audience loved it.

The night of the Orlando performance, Maggie was edgier than usual. Her hairstylist kept nagging at her to sit still. "Girlfriend, it's none of my business, but you sure have been restless lately."

"Cool it, Johnny."

"Just expressing concern. I hear there's a lot of money people out front." The hair dresser warmed to his favorite task—gossip. "They had a couple of huge dinners before the concert and brought a lot of those rich queens over in limos. Honey, you should see the gowns. And not all of them are on queens, mind you. There are some hot-looking women out there, too. Want me to scout one out for you? I have excellent taste in women."

"You probably have better luck with women than I do." Maggie laughed at the idea. "But tonight, I'll pass. I'm exhausted." Seeing the disappointment on his face, she added, "But maybe you can get some phone numbers for tomorrow. And don't forget the party at the hotel after the concert. Lots of food."

The concert started on time. Maggie was energized. She took a deep breath and ran out onto the stage. During the first set, she welcomed the local charities groups and asked the executive directors to come up on stage. Speaking strongly about the need to end AIDS, Maggie drew applause. "AIDS is not about being gay, being black, white, young, old. It's about being sick and wanting to live." The audience applauded loudly. She quieted the audience, then continued, "The Susan G. Komen Foundation has a special place in my heart. My mother died of breast cancer while still in her thirties, and it drastically changed my life. Her life was too short and I never got to really say good-bye." She began one of her new songs, a promise of hope in a lonely world.

As she finished, Maggie reached back near the edge of the band. A single yellow rose was given to each of the executive directors. As they were escorted off the stage, the audience stood and applauded, many wiping tears. It was the first time Maggie had publicly mentioned her mother. Two more songs and the first half of the performance ended with the band playing for several minutes before breaking. At intermission, she began to relax.

The last set was a slower pace, a combination of love songs and new music, including two more songs Maggie had completed during the tour. In spite of being hoarse and tired, this was her favorite part of the show.

She sat on the top step at the edge of the stage. Looking out into the dark arena, she spoke. "One of the many things I learned from a special person is that part of loving someone is finding magic and holding on to it, believing in it. This next song is a reminder that sometimes we have to work to find that magic."

The band began to play. Closing her eyes, M.J. slid a hand up and down her thigh. She hummed the melody. When she opened her eyes, she looked out into the black. "Tell that person that the love you feel deep inside will never go away, no matter what fears, no matter what threats and words they may hurl at you."

The lights dimmed and a soft, wailing sound began. Maggie closed her eyes as if she was lost in some other place, some other feeling. She began her new song, "Deep Inside Me." The words floated out hauntingly. A pain rose inside her every time she sang it, an ache so deep it permeated every cell of her body, reminding her of Susan and the emptiness in her life without Susan.

> My life was shadows
> Afraid to feel the flame
> Coldness numbed my heart
> And no one was the blame.
> I hid from love
> Unsure of what to do
> With all the pain inside
> Until there was you.

At the beginning of the song, she walked down the stairs to find someone to sing to. On the aisle in the fourth row the woman who haunted her awaited. Susan.

Maggie stumbled over the words, unable to discern fantasy and reality. Fearing she was hallucinating, she leaned close and whispered, "Susan?"

"Hello, Maggie," came the awkward reply. That wonderful voice filled Maggie with longing.

Taking Susan's hand, Maggie gently walked her up to the stairs. For the first time in months, Maggie felt hope. Her heart recognized the love and desire for Susan. She knew she couldn't lose her again.

Nodding to the band, Maggie began to sing again as they sat on the top step. Knees touching, Maggie looked into Susan's beautiful shimmering eyes. She looked at Susan and continued singing.

> You whispered my name
> While chasing away the dark
> I felt my life begin
> When you captured my heart.
> You reached deep inside me
> And set me on fire
> My soul set free
> My passion driven even higher
> Lay down beside me
> Stay deep inside me

Maggie's voice was husky and breathy, almost a whisper. Running a hand slowly down one thigh, Maggie leaned her head to one side, a long, low groan slowly slipping from her lips. She was one with the music. Susan felt the frost in her heart melting. Emotion was gaining some purchase in her life.

> I built fences to keep
> Anyone from getting near
> I've been trapped
> Inside my own chains of fear.
> This is the road more traveled
> With no one to guide me

The pain and want brought tears to Susan's eyes. Tears rolled down her cheeks.

> I am no longer alone
> With you deep inside me.
> Lay beside me,
> Teach me how to live.
> Let me dwell in the warmth of your love

I have so much to give.
With you deep inside me
My spirit can fly
There is nothing you ask
My heart won't try
With you beside me;
So deep inside me.

The last line was breathy, softer, seductive, like the first calm breath after an orgasm. The music ended and seconds passed before the crowd responded. The audience was wild, demanding an encore.

Maggie hesitated. She looked into Susan's eyes, questioning. She squeezed Susan's hand, relishing the feel of the soft flesh. "I love you," Maggie mouthed. A gentle nod and a smile from Susan and she agreed, reluctantly, to let go of Susan's hand. Moving the microphone to ensure privacy, she asked, "Will you wait up here on the stage for me? Please?"

Susan agreed. Only Maggie filled the vacuum in her life. Without the vibrant, passionate Maggie, her life had returned to the calm, prosaic existence she had wanted. And now hated.

Holding to Susan with one hand, Maggie lifted the microphone with the other and hummed the opening chords of the next song. Her music oozed sexuality. For once, her words reflected the emotion filling her.

Susan felt herself falling headlong into the whirlwind. Maggie's large hand came up, gently touching Susan's face. *Those glorious hands*, Susan thought, as she leaned into the touch.

By the end of the song, the audience had been wrapped in a cocoon of sex and promise. They were insatiable. Maggie wanted only to be with Susan. After the second encore, she led Susan down to her dressing room.

"What are you doing here? How did... I have so many questions. Oh, God, I'm just glad to see you." Maggie stopped.

"I'm rambling. Let me shower and change clothes. Have breakfast with me."

Before she could respond, Maggie shook her head. "Damn, I forgot. There's a fund-raiser at the hotel. I'm sorry. I want so much to talk to you." She laughed. "Alone. Would you mind joining me for a little while, and then I promise you I'll be yours. We don't leave town until day after tomorrow." Not waiting for an answer, she kissed her and felt the heat of the touch. "God, I've missed you."

Pushing back, Susan stared at the form-fitting jeans and bright red T-shirt. She looks great, Susan thought. The emotions running around inside her were dominated by one overwhelming feeling—being with Maggie. "I...I came here with a group of people from the Susan G. Komen fund-raiser. They're expecting me to have breakfast with them. I can't just walk out on them, but I definitely want to be with you."

"Tell them I'll take you back to the hotel, or to your house. Or wherever you want to go. Even better, invite them to join us." Maggie took a deep breath and felt hope fill her lungs. "I'm having breakfast catered. We can get more food. It's a fund-raiser for the Safehouse. We can call and get it arranged. Whatever it costs."

"Let's go ask." Susan held out her hand.

The group from the GLBT center waited near the stage, surprised that one of their members had disappeared with M.J. Carson. Susan approached them, still holding Maggie's hand. "Ms. Carson has invited us to join her at a fund-raiser breakfast for SafeHouse." She turned back to Maggie and began to introduce each person.

"Hi, how are you?" Maggie put out her hand greeting each person. The M.J. Carson charm worked. "Susan has graciously agreed to join me for breakfast and I would like you to join us. Will you, please?"

The group eagerly accepted Maggie's offer. After they

received instructions to her hotel, the group left the arena. Susan had clearly gained new prominence in the eyes of the group. They were ecstatic to be spending time in the company of the well-known star.

Taking Susan's hand, Maggie walked back to her dressing room. Maggie's voice was low and Susan strained to listen. "I owe you an apology."

The look on Maggie's face revealed more than any words. Susan could see that this was probably the hardest thing she had ever done. She wanted to reach out and reassure Maggie, but she hesitated. *What am I afraid of? I need to know she loves me and wants me as much as I do her.*

Maggie struggled for a place to begin. "Thank you for being here. For agreeing to spend this time with me. I've always thought you were the braver and stronger one."

And I always thought you the braver and stronger, Susan thought. She sat in a nearby chair.

"Susan, you walked into my crazy life, at times under duress, and loved me. For me." She paused, closing her eyes, struggling. "Even from the first, I've not always been honest or loving. At times, I've been a bitch and didn't even deserve your friendship." Maggie finally opened her eyes, her expression pleading. "I know you told me you loved me, but I kept…I waited for you to want something…or to leave me. I didn't trust your love because I didn't trust that I was lovable. I wouldn't blame you if you don't want to ever see me. I want you to know that I…" She tried to speak but emotion took over.

Susan stared down at her hands. Her head and heart were again at war, but it was her heart that yelled louder. A hand resting on her knee forced her to look up.

Maggie knelt in front of Susan. She carefully searched her face, looking for any encouragement. "I have loved only one woman. In the last five years, I have been involved with one, and only one, woman. The only woman I ever want in my life. I love you. It's stupid it should be so difficult for me to say that, but I do love you, only you."

Maggie clasped Susan's hand between hers. "Any plans, dreams, I have are about you, about us. You have the power to make me happy or destroy me. That scares the hell out of me. I am ashamed for the way I have treated you. I can't forgive myself and I don't expect you to forgive me. I don't know if…"

Maggie stopped. She looked briefly for encouragement. "I don't want to think of my life without you, but I…" She swallowed hard. "I will if that's what you choose. I'm still learning about love. I don't come with any guarantees, but I would like another chance."

Maggie was only inches away, but it seemed like the Grand Canyon to Susan. She imagined life without her. It wasn't hard. It was what she had been bemoaning for the last few months. Then she imagined life with Maggie. Chaotic, unpredictable, hills and valleys. And magic. Susan's own bonds began to crumble.

Maggie pulled Susan up. They stood with their hands together briefly before Maggie spoke. "I love you, Susan Hettinger. With all that I am and ever hope to be, I love you. As much as I have fought commitment, I know one thing: I want you in my life. For the rest of my life. I want to wake up next to you and grow old with you. I want to watch our children grow up happier than we did. I want to play in the sunshine with you and hold hands under the stars. I want to watch lines settle around your beautiful eyes and hear you complain about getting old. I want to wake up next to you until it is time for me to go to sleep for the last time. And then I want to lie in your arms and know I have been loved. The thought of you leaving scares the hell out of me. The thought of never seeing you again is worse. I want to make our life work. Whatever it takes."

Susan allowed her heart to speak. Suddenly she understood the depth of that word—magic. And the freedom. Maggie caressed the side of Susan's face. Susan had such clarity and understanding, she wondered why it had taken so long. The night in Atlanta when Maggie sang to her. The time Maggie made in her chaotic day for the two of them. This woman had been saying "I love you" in the many little, and big, things she did. *And I've been too deaf and blind to notice, or want to notice.*

Susan lifted Maggie's hands to her lips and kissed them. "Have I ever told you that it was your hands that I fell in love with first?"

Maggie shook her head.

"My precious Maggie. Right now, I'm not even sure who I am. And I'm afraid too. It took a while to figure out, but eventually I realized you are like my mother in many ways. I've struggled to be just the opposite. To have control, to be in control. And you…" Susan felt Maggie's pulse racing. She pressed Maggie's hand against her cheek. Maggie's hand was trembling. She put her hand on top of Maggie's.

Maggie couldn't remember ever feeling this much joy. Her heart was going to float out of her body. She pulled Susan tight against her. "Yes, and me?"

Her touch, her voice, her hands, Susan thought. The passion, the gentleness, the playfulness, the friendship. There was so much about Maggie to love and so much yet to know. Susan acknowledged that Maggie had won her heart that night on the plane. And now she held Maggie's heart in her hands. Staring into those wonderful eyes, she realized there was something magical about her, and she did not want to lose that. *Maggie has forever changed my life and I don't want to go back. I can't go back.*

"I love you," Maggie said.

"I love you too." Maggie had been saying that all along, and now Susan could hear it. *I am just as big a risk for Maggie—me and my need for control. Her chaos, my control. We might be able to make it work. How nice!*

I do believe in fairies!

EPILOGUE

Thanksgiving week, one year later

The lights dimmed and Maggie listened to her band play. Several bars into the opening number, the platform on which she stood slowly moved up, smoke and colored lights announcing her entrance. The crowd was wild. At last she was on stage. She sang and danced, happier than she had ever been.

"Thank you for being here tonight. Orlando always has such a great audience, and"—she looked down into the first row—"Orlando is my home because a certain woman in this town holds my heart." The crowd roared. Not long after the Orlando concert, Maggie and Derek held a press conference to talk about their private lives and to publicly come out. It had been such a freeing experience Maggie could no longer remember why she hadn't done it sooner. Derek, Paul, Maggie, and Susan were often seen together at a variety of events. All three children were happy in Florida, and Maggie and Susan were talking about more children.

The last year had been about growth…and love. For Maggie, the best part was the deepening love and strength she had found with Susan.

Looking out into the dark arena, she spoke. "One of the many things I learned from Susan is that part of loving someone is finding magic and holding on to it, believing in it. She was also the one to help me believe in magic. That magic is deep inside each of us, if we're just lucky enough to find it."

Susan sat where she did at every concert. She smiled. Maggie was her partner in every part of her life. She knew she had magic in her heart.

About the Author

C.J. Harte was born in New York but lived in many places courtesy of her father's military career. When her family finally settled in the South, she decided to attend college in Florida, where she obtained her degrees as well as a significant Southern accent and a unrelenting sense of humor.

C.J. has been a political activist and a community organizer, and was involved in professional organizations while maintaining a full-time job in health care. She edited a women's newspaper, wrote political editorials and satire, and was a speech writer for political candidates. She eventually climbed down the corporate ladder and moved out west. While she loves her day job, C.J.'s passion is her writing.

When not working or writing, C.J. is either commuting between continents or spending time with her four-footed friends in her beloved Wyoming, looking out at the mountains and blue sky.

Books Available From Bold Strokes Books

Magic of the Heart by C.J. Harte. CEO Susan Hettinger and wild, impulsive rock star M.J. Carson couldn't be more different if they tried—but opposites attract in ways neither woman can resist. (978-1-60282-131-6)

Ambereye by Gill McKnight. Jolie Garoul is falling in love with her assistant. The big problem is, Jolie is a werewolf. (978-1-60282-132-3)

Collision Course by C.P. Rowlands. Tragedy leaves Brie O'Malley and Jordan Carter fearful and alone. Can they find the courage to take a second chance on love? (978-1-60282-133-0)

Mephisto Aria by Justine Saracen. Opera singer Katherina Marov's destiny may be to repeat the mistakes of her father when she becomes involved in a dangerous love affair. (978-1-60282-134-7)

Battle Scars by Meghan O'Brien. Returning Iraq war veteran Ray McKenna struggles with the battle scars that can only be healed by love. (978-1-60282-129-3)

Chaps by Jove Belle. Eden Metcalf wants nothing more than to flee from her troubled past and travel the open road—until she runs into rancher Brandi Cornwell. (978-1-60282-127-9)

Lightbearer by John Caruso. Lucifer dares to question the premise of creation itself and reveals that sin may be all that stands between us and living hell. (978-1-60282-130-9)

The Seeker by Ronica Black. FBI profiler Kennedy Scott battles ghosts from her past, deadly obsession, and the evil that haunts her. (978-1-60282-128-6)

Power Play by Julie Cannon. Businesswomen Tate Monroe and Victoria Sosa are at odds in the boardroom, but not in the bedroom. (978-1-60282-125-5)

The Remarkable Journey of Miss Tranby Quirke by Elizabeth Ridley. When love enters Tranby's life in the form of a beautiful nineteen-year-old student, Lysette McDonald, she embarks on the most remarkable journey of all. (978-1-60282-126-2)

Returning Tides by Radclyffe. Insurance investigator Ashley Walker faces more than a dangerous opponent when she returns to the town, and the woman, she left behind. (978-1-60282-123-1)

Veritas by Anne Laughlin. When the hallowed halls of academia become the stage for murder, newly appointed Dean Beth Ellis's search for the truth leads her to unexpected discoveries about her own heart. (978-1-60282-124-8)

The Pleasure Planner by Larkin Rose. Pleasure purveyor Bree Hendricks treats love like a commodity until Logan Delaney makes Bree the client in her own game. (978-1-60282-121-7)

everafter by Nell Stark and Trinity Tam. Valentine Darrow is bitten by a vampire on her way to propose to her lover Alexa Newland, and their lives and love are placed in mortal jeopardy. (978-1-60282-119-4)

Summer Winds by Andrews & Austin. When Maggie Turner hires a ranch hand to help work her thousand acres, she never expects to be attracted to the very young, very female Cash Tate. (978-1-60282-120-0)

Beggar of Love by Lee Lynch. Jefferson is the lover every woman wants to be—or to have. A revealing saga of lesbian sexuality. (978-1-60282-122-4)

The Seduction of Moxie by Colette Moody. When 1930s Broadway actress Violet London meets speakeasy singer Moxie Valette, she is instantly attracted and her Hollywood trip takes an unexpected turn. (978-1-60282-114-9)

Goldenseal by Gill McKnight. When Amy Fortune returns to her childhood home, she discovers something sinister in the air—but is former lover Leone Garoul stalking her or protecting her? (978-1-60282-115-6)

Romantic Interludes 2: Secrets edited by Radclyffe and Stacia Seaman. An anthology of sensual lesbian love stories: passion, surprises, and secret desires. (978-1-60282-116-3)

Femme Noir by Clara Nipper. Nora Delaney meets her match in Max Abbott, a sex-crazed dame who may or may not have the information Nora needs to solve a murder—but can she contain her lust for Max long enough to find out? (978-1-60282-117-0)

The Reluctant Daughter by Lesléa Newman. Heartwarming, heartbreaking, and ultimately triumphant—the story every daughter recognizes of the lifelong struggle for our mothers to really see us. (978-1-60282-118-7)

Erosistible by Gill McKnight. When Win Martin arrives at a luxurious Greek hotel for a much-anticipated week of sun and sex with her new girlfriend, she is stunned to find her ex-girlfriend, Benny, is the proprietor. Aeros Ebook. (978-1-60282-134-7)

Looking Glass Lives by Felice Picano. Cousins Roger and Alistair become lifelong friends and discover their sexuality amidst the backdrop of twentieth-century gay culture. (978-1-60282-089-0)

Breaking the Ice by Kim Baldwin. Nothing is easy about life above the Arctic Circle—except, perhaps, falling in love. At least that's what pilot Bryson Faulkner hopes when she meets Karla Edwards. (978-1-60282-087-6)

It Should Be a Crime by Carsen Taite. Two women fulfill their mutual desire with a night of passion, neither expecting more until law professor Morgan Bradley and student Parker Casey meet again…in the classroom. (978-1-60282-086-9)

Rough Trade edited by Todd Gregory. Top male erotica writers pen their own hot, sexy versions of the term "rough trade," producing some of the hottest, nastiest, and most dangerous fiction ever published. (978-1-60282-092-0)

The High Priest and the Idol by Jane Fletcher. Jemeryl and Tevi's relationship is put to the test when the Guardian sends Jemeryl on a mission that puts her not only in harm's way, but back into the sights of a previous lover. (978-1-60282-085-2)

MAGIC
OF THE HEART

Visit us at www.boldstrokesbooks.com